For Thom, my forever love
and the source of much inspiration.

"When the Moon Winks *is surprising and unpredictable, always funny and entertaining. Helen wrestles with challenges and becomes a whole woman, traveling from sadness to joy, learning to be open to her life. And yes, the resolution will warm your heart—it is true to life with more than one hilarious bump in the road.*"

–HAZEL DAWKINS, AUTHOR OF THE
DR. YOKO MYSTERY, *EYE WITNESS*

"When the Moon Winks *is a story that will make you laugh, shake your head at Helen, and reflect on your own choices … and leave you watching for the moon to wink.*"

–NANCY LiPETRIE, AUTHOR OF
THE WOODED PATH AND *ACROSS THE LAKE*

"*… had me on Chapter 1. I couldn't wait to find out what Helen had gotten herself into next. Just like the first book,* Where the Wind Blows *is a page-turner … I'm waiting for book three and more!*"

–JANE KORN

"*Although* Where the Wind Blows *is mainly light-hearted, it does leave the reader with plenty to think about … Like Helen, the reader is reminded to try and let go and see where life leads her … You are sure to be thinking about the message of this book for some time. I highly recommend it!*"

–DONNA MILLIGAN

Where the Wind Blows

A Novel

Hope Andersen

ISBN: 978-1-957723-31-0

Andersen. Hope
Where the Wind Blows

Edited by: Amy Ashby

Published by WARREN Publishing
Charlotte, NC
www.warrenpublishing.net
Printed in the United States

Acknowledgments

I want to thank a number of people who have contributed to the production of *Where the Wind Blows*. First, I'd like to thank all those who read *When the Moon Winks* and encouraged me to write a sequel. That you were taken in by Helen and her story gave me the encouragement to continue her tale, though that was never really in question as the previous novel left on a cliffhanger!

I'd also like to thank my early reviewers—Jane Korn and Donna Milligan—who gave their time to read the final draft and write something up for me. I know how busy you both are and I truly appreciate your taking the time and showing interest.

It almost goes without saying that I am indebted to Amy Ashby, my editor at Warren Publishing, for doing such a grand job, as she always does, whipping my books into shape. And to Mindy Kuhn, president of Warren Publishing and book designer extraordinaire, for fabricating yet another enchanting cover and for designing a beautiful interior to my novel.

Thanks always to my daughters and son who encouraged me to continue on this writing journey, and to my ever-supportive husband, Thom, who indulges me in every way.

Finally, thanks to you whoever you are, for picking up *Where the Wind Blows* and devoting your precious time to reading my creation. I am humbled by your attention.

Where the Wind Blows

Chapter 1

On New Year's Eve, Helen Ferry sat on the velvet sofa in front of a dying fire, ruminating on the last year. The ball in Times Square had just dropped, and 2020 was ushered in. For Helen, 2019 had been one of those years full of unexpected, and sometimes unwanted, twists and turns. On the bright side, her first grandchild, Frankie, had been born just before Christmas. On the downside, her ex-husband Frank was killed in a car crash on the way to the birthing center that night. Back to the bright side, she had grown closer to Gerard Ferguson, the charming Welshman with whom she had fallen in love. Bad side, the entrance of a new virus scientists had not yet identified. But back to Gerard ….

At first just a colleague on sabbatical from abroad, Gerard had become more than a friend since his arrival the year before. Were Helen being honest with herself, she had to admit she had fallen for him the moment he walked into her office and suggested they go for tea. But that was months ago, months of shy flirtation and frustrating courtship. Didn't he understand that at sixty-one, she didn't have that much time? Or was he just toying with her? That was her biggest fear. That he was just toying with her and never meant to be involved.

Recently, he had asked her to travel to Wales to spend Christmas with him. Helen, who had acquiesced and enjoyed the trip immensely, convinced herself their relationship could never work and nipped it in the bud. He was lost to her forever. Bright side, she was still employed, somewhat of a celebrity in academic worlds as a Shakespearian scholar. She had a wonderful cottage on the Long Island Sound and a precious puppy named Perdita. Downside, she was alone on New Year's Eve. The last she had seen of her old neighbor, Gloria, was when her friend had driven off in a red Corvette with an octogenarian named Everett. And her friends, Ron and Lou, had moved to California.

The flames in the fire were bright enough to pick up the red highlights in her mane of hair and to catch the gold in her green eyes. She was slim and movie-star beautiful. "What a lot of good that's done me," Helen said aloud as a self-pitying tear dropped into her champagne flute. "This is not the New Year's Eve I would have imagined for myself at this time of my life," she said softly because her daughter and son-in-law and three-week-old granddaughter were sleeping in the adjacent rooms. Helen had invited them to leave their small apartment behind for the holidays and spend time with her at the cottage. They happily accepted and were grateful for both the space and the help with the infant, whose sleep patterns were erratic to say the least. On New Year's Eve, they excused themselves early and crept off to bed at about 9 p.m., knowing the baby was sure to wake them in the middle of the night. So, Helen was alone.

She had not anticipated being alone. Really, she had brought it on herself. Not trusting her relationship with Gerard had any chance of working out, she had left him in Wales and cried all the way back to the United States. "Why couldn't I have let well enough alone?" Helen asked herself, as she had several hundred times since her return. This was the final straw. She would never forgive herself for being such an ass. If she died an old woman without a significant other, well, she deserved it for being so controlling and cautious.

In a moment of clarity, Helen realized all this bad talk was the booze speaking, and the best thing she could do would be to take herself to bed. There had been no watching the ball drop in Times Square with Gerard as she had hoped. They were just not destined for each other—3,000 miles apart and a nineteen-year difference in age. He was moving into the prime of his life while she was on the downswing.

"*Stop!*" Helen told the champagne that was lubricating her morose thoughts. But she poured herself another drink anyway just because there was no one here with her on New Year's Eve. Nor ever would be, as far as she could tell. So why not get drunk and pass out on the sofa? "Because that would upset Grace," Helen told herself, thinking of her only child. She rose, gulping down the last of the bubbly, and brought the glass to the sink where she set it down. Then she began her ascent up to her bedroom on the second floor.

Suddenly, she heard something.

In the still, cold dark, she heard a scratching at the front door, as if someone were trying to pick the lock and get in. Probably just an animal searching for warmth, she assured herself. But the scratching grew louder, and Helen's thoughts escalated from thinking maybe it was just mischief-makers to a serial killer on the loose. Whomever was trying to get in certainly wasn't subtle. They knocked into the rope of Indian prayer bells she had placed on the door and set them ringing. Helen ran down the stairs into the kitchen, reached down into a cupboard, and grabbed the most effective weapon she had in the house—a cast-iron skillet she had inherited from her grandmother. Then, she quickly scooted over by the door, prepared to knock the intruder on the head as soon as he entered her home.

Slowly, the door opened. A blast of cold air came through as a giant figure in black loomed in the doorway, blowing streams of air through his nostrils like some mythological bull. Helen prepared to attack but faltered as a familiar voice spoke out to her through her drunken haze.

"Well, are you going to ask me in? It's bloody cold out here," Gerard Ferguson, the Welshman who had stolen her heart, spoke through chattering teeth. "I tried my spare key, but the lock was iced over."

Helen Ferry stood at the front door of her cottage. The snow had stopped, and the temperatures dropped to well below freezing. She was looking into the face of the man she loved, whom she thought she had lost forever. But here he was, tall, dark, and more handsome than she remembered, waiting for her to invite him in. *Is it possible*, she thought, *that he can really be here, or is this some champagne-induced hallucination? It is, after all, New Year's Eve.* The stars were so clear in the brittle winter sky, they looked as if they might shatter at the slightest sound. Certainly, the *Hallelujah*! that was welling up inside her would usher their demise. The timbre of his deep voice and the lilt of his accent erased any doubt this might just be a fantasy, her New Year's wish.

"How did you …Why are you …." she stammered, but Gerard put an end to her questioning as he took her in his arms and kissed her passionately.

"Couldn't start a new year without that," he grinned. "A good surprise?"

Helen nodded. *The best*, she thought.

But," she cautioned as she took his arm to go into the warm house, "be very quiet. Grace and Jake are here, and Frankie is sleeping in the nursery."

"Quiet as a mouse," he whispered, following her into the living room where the embers of the fire shone like rubies and the white lights on the Christmas tree set all the glass ornaments and tinsel on the tree sparkling.

They sat down on the sofa, next to each other, not touching, while Helen held her breath, searching for the right questions to ask. Why had he come? Was it the whim of a lonely bachelor? What did he want? What did he hope for? And what about her? Could she really open her heart? He lived so far away. And what of the age difference? She was nineteen years older than he. Too late. It was already done. She had fallen for him. Hard. Now what was he going to do?

She glanced over at him expectantly, wishing he could only read what was in her heart. Her answer came quickly as he took both her hands in his and kissed them. "You are my New Year's wish. I want to spend this year, every year, with you." Then he leaned over and kissed her again so deeply, she could barely breathe. *To hell with suffocating or roasting up with passion*, Helen thought. This was what she wanted for New Year's too.

Chapter 2

January 1, 2020

No one could have been more surprised than Helen the next morning when she woke from what she had thought was a delicious dream to Gerard lying in bed beside her. She peeked under the covers and saw she was entirely naked, pulled the sheets and blankets up to her chin, and considered her next move. She wanted to make a dash to the master bath where her cozy bathrobe hung on a peg on the wall, but to get there, she needed coverage. The last thing she wanted was for her daughter and granddaughter to pay her an early morning surprise visit, only to find Grandma in her birthday suit and a man in bed beside her. Most likely in his birthday suit too. She didn't dare look.

Helen spotted the chenille blanket Grace had given her for Christmas, the softest gray with red cardinals imprinted all over it and a flurry of snowflakes. She grabbed it and wrapped herself warmly in the throw. Then she made a beeline for the bathroom and quickly covered herself with her robe, leaving the blanket in a puddle on the floor. She assessed her situation as she looked at herself in the mirror. *I've slept with Gerard. At least it appears that I have slept with Gerard. All the evidence points to that. Why don't I remember? What do I remember?* Helen asked herself. Vague fragments of the night before returned to her, glinting like slivers of mica on the solid gray of her memory. She remembered his walking in and the kiss. And then, champagne. Of course, more champagne. And then, nothing. Just waking up this morning deliciously warm after a perfect sleep. Until—until what? Until nothing, just she lying naked next to a man she had known for fifteen months, desired for as many, but kept a distance from until fairly recently. And now this.

Helen picked up her electric toothbrush, as if on autopilot, and went at it. Then she scrubbed her face to within an inch of its life and fiercely brushed her auburn hair, which she then snugged up in a shower cap. She turned the faucets to blazing hot and stepped into the water, wanting, and not wanting, to wash away last night's sex. A stranger might have thought she was punishing herself, and in a way, she was. She was beating herself up for having given in. All this could bring was trouble and hurt. At least, that was what she told herself as she stepped out of the shower, dried herself off, and tried to apply just enough cosmetics to make herself look a bit younger. God knows she was acting that way.

Many thoughts crossed Helen's mind as she outlined her eyes in thin strokes of deep gray. How was she going to tell Grace Gerard had flown in from Wales and spent the night in her bed? Grace would want to know where all this would lead. She would either throw a fit or leap ahead to Helen selling the house by Monday and moving 10,000 miles away next week, never to see her granddaughter again.

Helen placed her knuckles firmly on the sink and scolded herself in the mirror. "Stop being such a fool," she said to her reflection. "You are a grown woman. You can do whatever you please. Besides, if you are lucky, Gerard will find a position here."

Suddenly, the mirror was filled with the image of an almost-naked man standing behind her. Her heart skipped when she caught sight of his broad shoulders, muscles cut, as they would say at the gym. An image of him hovering over her, making love to her, those same muscles flexing, made her blush. She turned her eyes away. He had put on his black boxers, out of modesty.

"Gerard will find what?" he asked, placing his hands on her shoulders and kissing her neck, which sent shivers all through Helen.

"Nothing. Just thinking aloud. It is all so complicated."

"Should I not have come?"

"Oh no, no! I am so glad that you did, that you are here! It's just Grace …."

As if on cue, Grace knocked on the bedroom door, calling out. "Mommy? Mom? Are you awake? Someone wants to see you. Can we come in?"

Without even waiting for a response, Grace entered the room, carrying baby Frankie in her arms. She looked around and didn't see her mother anywhere. Helen was frantically trying to convince Gerard to hide in the shower. Gerard was not amused.

"Coming," Helen trilled to Grace as she flushed the toilet for effect, then emerged from the bathroom, blushing and breathless.

"Wow, Mom," Grace said. "You look exhausted. That must have been some—"

"Night," Gerard completed her thought as he emerged from the bathroom with Helen's patterned throw draped over his shoulders. He looked like a drag queen or, alternately, the Mikado.

"Mom! Gerard!" Grace shrieked.

Helen just closed her eyes.

"She had to find out sometime," Gerard murmured in Helen's ear.

"Find out what?" Grace asked.

"This." Gerard got down on one knee in front of the baffled Helen, took her right hand in his, and slipped a shiny gold bracelet onto her wrist. "Helen Ferry, will you be my best girl?"

Helen felt the blood rise to her face like mercury. All she could think was *Where did he hide that thing*? She was desperately trying to block all other thoughts out of her mind.

"There's an inscription." Gerard pointed to the phrase on the slim bangle. It read, "never, never, never give up." Winston Churchill to the troops. Helen was disappointed. First, this hadn't been a proper marriage proposal though, honestly, she didn't know what she would have done with that. Second, he had chosen a rather overworked slogan to express how he felt. Never give up? Did that mean there had been a time when he thought he might but hadn't? Did it mean he thought her so impossible, he couldn't ask the big question, but he would keep on trying? Helen would have preferred a line from Dylan Thomas's poetry, a reminder of the days they had spent in Wales together when it was clear they had fallen in love. Even if he had just said, "to my Caitlin." She had such hopes he'd be a sentimental man.

"You're disappointed," he said, breaking into her reverie.

"Not at all! Not at all. It's lovely."

"I'd have used something from Dylan Thomas, but his lines are all so bloody long. I would have had to buy you a long necklace."

"Don't be silly. It's perfect."

"You will then? Be my best girl?"

"Of course, I will."

Then Gerard rose and kissed her, tipping her chin up toward him. The towel slipped from his shoulders as he took her in his arms.

Grace stood by the door to the bedroom, unable to move. But she could cry, and that she did, steady tears running down her cheeks, making her nose run. She had never seen her mother happier or more beautiful, and that made Grace both pleased and sad. She wondered if her mother had spent all those years in an unhappy marriage to Frank Court just for her daughter, to keep the pretense of a normal family intact.

Whatever Helen had now with Gerard was special. Grace could see it, feel it. Their love was palpable. So what if Helen was sixty-one and Gerard only forty-two? Plenty of relationships worked when there was an age difference. Wouldn't his youth and virility keep her mother younger longer? Grace shuddered a little, not really wanting to imagine her mother's sex life, but glad for her if she had a robust one. But what about the travel? Gerard lived in Wales while Helen was firmly ensconced with family, house, and job here in Connecticut. She couldn't just up and walk away? Or could she? Would she? These were modern times. Surely, Grace, who had the lion's share of attachments, would call the shots. After all, she and Jake were counting on Helen to watch Frankie when they went away for a few days now and then. Surely, her mother wouldn't forgo her role as Grandmother.

The baby stirred in Grace's arms, looking up at her mother with the milky blue eyes of an infant. Her little bow mouth popped open and shut like a baby bird. Before Frankie had time to work herself into a frenzy, Grace walked downstairs to the nursery and sat in the white rocking chair. She pulled open her nightshirt and helped the baby clamp on to her oversized breast, now swollen hard with milk.

Grace sat in the quiet room, watching the dancing swirls of light on the ceiling. They came from the honeybee carousel Helen had bought for Frankie. This whole nursery had been her mother's dream. A honey-colored room full of happy Pooh Bear images, and quilts and rugs fashioned in warm, soft pastels, her mom had created a sanctuary for her granddaughter. A place of beauty where she could feel comfortable, safe, and loved.

To make up for me, thought Grace, whose first "bedroom" had been a walk-in closet in Helen and Frank's small townhouse, and whose life had only *appeared* comfortable and safe. In truth, it never had been. Her dad, the mortician, was dull and uninspired. Grace always smelled death on him, though he covered it up with a sweet cologne and antiseptic cleanser. Her mother was so preoccupied with her work and her appearance, she barely seemed to notice Grace growing up. As if to make up for their inadequacies, they sent her to boarding school in grade nine. If there ever were family times, they usually ended in arguments, or worse still, they passed like an iceberg in a slow, stony silence that chilled Grace to the bone.

After the divorce, which came as a relief to Grace, Helen changed, underwent a transformation really. Grace attributed this largely to Sylvia, the old woman who ran a rental home where they had stayed for Christmas a year ago. Sylvia was the one who encouraged Helen to work on herself "from the inside out." It was because of Sylvia Helen had bought this house on the beach and turned it into a haven of serenity, complete with the lovely nursery Grace now sat in. It was because of Sylvia Helen was open to "wait and see" with Gerard.

And now this. Asked to go steady on New Year's Day! Grace hoped and prayed Helen didn't return to the old Helen who had been all about having things go her own way. Grace was fairly certain her mother would have preferred a more solid arrangement, a marriage proposal even. Something with heft and title, where she would be able to maintain some control. This loose-goosey steady thing might just be the spring that burst forth and sent Helen scrambling, chasing Gerard, following him wherever he would have her go until he finally came to his senses and bought her an expensive ring.

Grace prayed her mother would remember her life was first and foremost intricately involved with Grace's life too. And while it might seem fun to just up and move to Wales with her new boyfriend, to be in a new and exciting romance, she had responsibilities at home with her daughter and granddaughter. She couldn't just leave. Or could she? Would she?

Grace found herself crying again, this time not over the sweet intensity of the love she had witnessed between her mother and Gerard, but because she felt sad. More than sad, abandoned and afraid. Just when she thought her life was finally smoothing out, that there were days of peace and joy ahead, this happened. It all went to shit.

As soon as she had that thought, a more reasonable idea appeared. It was something she had told her mother repeatedly during her hard times. Helen thought it sounded like a fortune cookie reading, but to Grace it was profound: "No expectations, no disappoints." So that was how she decided to handle all this business with Helen and Gerard. To bring no expectations. To suffer no disappointments.

The baby had fallen off Grace's nipple and was sleeping again. Grace closed her shirt, smoothed Frankie's brown hair away from her eyes, and laid her down in her crib. As she tucked a little yellow blanket around the sleeping child, Grace smiled. *It's all good*, she told herself. *It's all good*.

By the time Helen and Gerard emerged downstairs, hair still damp from the shower and smelling of vanilla and jasmine, Grace was already hard at work fixing breakfast. She had sausages browning in a skillet, aromatic coffee in the French press, cinnamon buns in the oven, and eggs scrambling in another pan. A quartet of juice glasses, decorated with bright red roosters, the ones Helen and Grace had purchased at IKEA, were filled with orange juice. Everything smelled and looked delicious, like Christmas morning.

Helen watched her daughter with awe. How far Grace had come from the exuberant adolescent, clanging pots and pans around and leaving a mess for someone else to clean up, to this proficient chef, cleaning as she went, miraculously making everything come out like clockwork. *She is such an amazing girl … amazing woman,* Helen thought, correcting herself. *An amazing woman with a husband and child. A husband!* Helen smiled. Maybe she would have a husband again, though she really didn't feel the need. Being Gerard's "best girl" was good enough for now. Though, he had hinted in the shower that he hoped for more.

Call me old-fashioned, Helen thought, *or maybe uptight, but the age difference is a factor.* If they did marry, and soon, how long would their marriage last? Fifteen years? Twenty? When she died, he would be in his sixties. Not a bad age for a man to remarry—if he aged well, which she was certain Gerard would. Look at him now! She felt a little guilt at robbing him of opportunities with younger women. Even as the thoughts passed through her mind, Helen knew they were ridiculous. Gerard loved her, and she loved him. If they had fifteen wonderful years together, well glory hallelujah! That was longer than many marriages lasted these days.

She was reminded of Micah, her friend and antiques dealer, and his husband Nicholas. Theirs was a marriage with an age difference. Nicholas was younger than Gerard— and an actor! But they seemed so happy, devoted to each other. It gave her hope. Ironically, last Christmas, when she had visited Micah over the holiday, fully expecting their old romance to be rekindled, the "boys" and Grace had teased her about expecting an engagement ring from her old beau. She had thought she was ready then. She thought she knew with whom. Little did she know that all this would transpire. But life has a way of doing that. As Grace always said, "If you send your dreams out into the Universe, they have a way of coming true." Helen was a believer now. Maybe the bracelet wasn't a diamond ring, but Gerard's message was clear: He would never give up until she was his. It was just a matter of the right time.

Grace's voice interrupted Helen's thoughts.

"Mom, can you go get Jake and Frankie? I don't know what's taking him so long, and the eggs are ready."

Gerard gave Helen's hand a squeeze as she walked off to find her son-in-law and granddaughter.

Jake wasn't in the guest room, where the bed was already made neat and tidy, or the guest bath. Surely, he wouldn't have gone up to her suite. She looked in the library. Maybe he was searching out a good book. But he wasn't there. The room was still, and dust motes sparkled as the morning sun poured in on the paperwhites she had forced in a rectangular glass container. Helen paused, taking in the stillness. She loved this house, so cozy with the snow blanketing the lawn outside and dangling in great drops from the trees. Every once in a while, a handful would fall, and the snow would shake down in a fine powder.

"*Mom!*" Grace shrieked from the kitchen.

Helen hustled back to her quest. The only place left, really the first place she should have looked, was the nursery. She found Jake there, standing at the edge of the crib and looking down on his little girl. She was curled up like a comma, thumb almost in her mouth, her breathing steady. Every once in a while, a little smile and a squeal emerged, which made Jake smile too. Helen didn't have the heart to tell him she was just passing gas.

"Isn't she perfection?" he asked quietly.

"She is."

"I can't believe she is really here."

"She is."

They were quiet for a moment. Helen felt happiness like she had never known before. Here was a man who loved her daughter, truly loved her, and loved his daughter more. She, too, loved the baby girl, her daughter, and Jake, and Gerard, and herself. She felt positively obese with love, as if she might explode any minute! But then her stomach growled and reminded her how empty she really was.

"Breakfast is ready. Let's go eat," she told him. They closed the door to the nursery quietly behind them as they left.

When they entered the kitchen, Jake did a double-take upon seeing Gerard at the table.

"Whoa, man, look who the cat dragged in! Gerard, how are you doing?" he exclaimed.

"So, " Grace said to Jake as she served him eggs and sausage at the breakfast table. "You missed the exciting news."

"News? What news?" he asked, helping himself to a cinnamon bun still warm from the oven.

"Show him, Mom," Grace instructed.

Helen, blushing, held out her arm and pushed up her sleeve to reveal the gold bracelet.

"Nice. 'Never, never, never give up.' What's the occasion?" he asked.

"Gerard's asked me to be his 'best girl,'" Helen explained, pulling her sleeve down over her wrist.

"Cute," Jake commented. "What's the matter, Gerard? Couldn't spring for a ring?" Jake joked, winking at the older man.

Helen felt herself blush as Gerard worked his way around the table to come to her side. She felt embarrassed, partly for Gerard, who had just been delivered a not-so-subtle blow, and partly for herself, who had allowed this "going steady" charade in the first place. Mostly, she was embarrassed for

Jake, who had been so uncouth as to mouth his words. She was sure Grace would give him an earful later in the evening.

As if sensing her mood, Gerard put his arm around her shoulder and kissed the top of her head. "You Yanks are always in such a hurry," he said to Jake with a smile. "You of all people, Jake, with all your meditating and zen, should be aware of the value of giving things time. I look forward to a long, luscious courtship with Helen, during which I will do my best to convince her that she is the rare jewel I have always sought, my precious to whom I will pledge my life and all my belongings. And there is no shortage of that, I assure you. If I had a mind to, I could buy her a ring of great value, but I choose not to. I choose to 'go steady' and see where that takes us."

Helen felt the blood rushing up into her face. Perhaps Gerard had been wise to play with her this way. Maybe he knew she would think things through and realize she wanted to be with him no matter what.

"Honestly," he continued, "I don't care how long I have to wait, just as long as in the end, I will be with you forever."

"Now there's a proper answer," Helen said, kissing him lightly on the lips. "Eat your eggs."

New Year's Day passed uneventfully. They all pitched in, washing dishes and cleaning the kitchen. Gerard lit a fire in the hearth, which then instructed him to keep going all day long.

"Anything for you, darling," Gerard leaned over to kiss Helen's neck. She pushed him away, gently.

"Not in front of the others. It makes me feel uncomfortable."

Gerard stood back, perplexed, concern written over his face. "Are you embarrassed that I am so in love with you?"

"Not at all. I just don't want it to be awkward for them. You know, I am Grace's mother, for God's sake. Frankie's grandmother. I can't really run around acting like a teenage girl."

"It's the age thing, isn't it?" Gerard's voice was deep and dark.

"No! You could be forty-two or eighty-seven, and I'd still feel this way."

"More so, I should think." Gerard whispered. "Imagine falling for someone with dentures and a limp dick!"

"Gerard!" Helen sounded alarmed, though secretly, she was amused.

"At least you've made the better choice, opting for a young, virile lad like myself."

Helen thought of Micah and his relationship with Nicholas, so much younger and handsomer than he. They had been together for seven years now and, thanks to new laws, had been married for two of them. They were happy, though they had the odds stacked against them. Sometimes love and commitment were easier when there was an obstacle to overcome, a social more that stood like a guard dog gnarling at happiness. Love and commitment bound couples together.

"You are awfully quiet. That worries me."

"Not to worry," Helen said, squeezing Gerard's hand. "I am just thinking about some friends of mine who are in the same situation."

"What situation would that be?"

"You know. One older. One younger."

Gerard turned from Helen and knelt down in front of the fire. He opened the screen and started to poke at the logs that really didn't need any poking at all. Everything was very still except for the crackling of the fire and the sound of Grace and Jake as they gave Frankie a bath in her plastic tub.

"You are not going to let go of your reservations about the age thing, are you?" Gerard asked her at last.

"I am trying to."

"What is it then?"

Helen came and kneeled next to Gerard, resting her hands on his thighs. "So many things," she said. "I wonder most of all why you would fall for a woman my age. Is there something you are lacking? Something you want? Why me?"

Gerard looked at Helen for a moment, then took her face in his hands. "So, the age thing is a problem for you. It is not me who is lacking something. I have everything I could ever need. It's you. You just can't believe that someone could love you just as you are. No strings attached. No loops. Just me loving you. And I think that terrifies you."

"Baffles me. You could have a younger, more attractive woman."

Gerard shook his head in dismay. "You just don't get it, as they say here in America, do you? It's not your body I am after, it's your mind. I don't think I have ever met a woman with as brilliant a mind."

"What, you don't find me attractive?" Helen whined.

"You haven't heard a word I said. I love you for who you are on the inside. And yes, of course, I find you attractive." Gerard ran his fingers through his hair, exasperated. "You have told me about your friend Sylvia. Didn't she tell you that loving yourself was the most important thing you could do?" Helen nodded as she looked down at the bracelet sparkling in the firelight. "You know, you can give that thing back to me right now if you like. I can make this all disappear. But I warn you, if I walk out that door this time, I won't be coming back. I'll be finished for good."

Helen felt the heat rise in her chest, her breathing quickened, and tears welled up in her eyes. That was not what she wanted. That was not what she wanted at all, but she realized deep down that was what she expected. She expected to be left alone, abandoned. Suddenly, she felt like a drowning child, flailing her arms in the water with no one there at the surface to help her. She was gasping for air, but each gasp filled her lungs with water. Surely, she would drown.

Gerard put his arms around Helen and held her as she wept. She clung to him as to a life preserver that had been thrown to her. She didn't have words. She didn't know what to say. She just hoped he could feel through her heart the message she was trying desperately to send.

Gerard stroked her hair. "Shh," he soothed her. "Everything is all right. I'm not going anywhere. I love you."

❁

By the time Grace and Jake walked in with a spanking clean Frankie, all rosy and decked out in an adorable yellow onesie with a little hood and ears, Helen had gone back up back upstairs to "fix her face," though Gerard could see no need for that.

"Where's Mom?" Grace asked as she entered the room.

"She just went upstairs for a moment. That's a precious little dumpling you have in your arms. May I?" Gerard asked, reaching out to hold the baby. Grace placed Frankie carefully in Gerard's arms.

"Great! Now maybe I can do some stretches!" Grace said, reaching up toward the ceiling and stretching side to side.

"Stretch away! I'll hold her for as long as you desire."

Just then, Jake walked in with an armful of logs. "Thought we might need these. It has started snowing again."

"Cool! I want to take Frankie out in the snow," Grace said, speaking as she twisted gently.

"Make sure you bundle her up," cautioned Helen, who had emerged from upstairs, looking radiant and refreshed.

Gerard gazed on Helen, the love he felt for her evident in his eyes, then looked away. "I'll be happy to keep her snuggled up next to my chest. Just strap that harness on me, stuff her in her snowsuit and hat, and she'll be cozy as a ladybug on a summer's day."

"Sounds good to me," Jake said, looking over at Grace.

"Sure," Grace agreed. "Let's get going before it turns into a blizzard." She took the baby from Gerard, cooing, "Little Frankie, let's get you in your snow sack and get you ready for Uncle … Grandpa … Gerard to take you for a walk."

At the word "Grandpa," Gerard's eyebrows rose, and a smile spread across his face. Helen knew he would never leave her now.

The brisk walk down to the beach and back did not turn out to be exactly what Grace had hoped for. The wind had picked up, and the snow blew horizontally on their faces, not big, puffy snowflakes but hard little pellets with an attitude, verging on sleet.

"Are you sure you want to do this, Grace?" Helen asked as she pulled her cashmere scarf up to her nose. "Do you think Frankie will be all right?"

Grace looked over at her possibly future stepfather. *How strange did that sound?* Gerard, a big man already, seemed large as a bear in his winter coat buttoned almost to the top. Generally fit, his belly now protruded with the lump created by the baby resting against his chest under his coat. His gloved hands rested on her back, giving extra protection. There was no way Frankie was anything but toasty in that ride.

"She's fine," Grace said. "Gerard's got her snuggled up in there. If anything, she may be too warm."

Helen smiled, trudging through the blistering snow, thankful she had worn sunglasses, silly as it seemed, the sky being so gray and all. One look at her daughter's eyes, the lashes laced with white, told her she had made a good choice.

The men were walking ahead next to the gunmetal gray water, its incoming waves fringed in white foam. *Such a far cry from summer,* Helen thought, remembering when she and Gerard had strolled along the beach looking for shells and sand dollars, and the terns ran frantically on toothpick legs, leaving V-shaped prints in the moist sand. Heaven it was, in summer. *But this is Heaven too*, Helen thought, *if you look at it the right way.* A gray and white version of a summer's day with a wind that brought roses to one's cheeks and made one's eyes tingle.

How exactly was this Heaven? Helen asked herself again. It was Heaven because she was here with her daughter and son-in-law, and her grandchild and boyfriend. Did she dare say it? Think it? Realize it? Her *boyfriend.* She hadn't had a boyfriend for more than forty years. It seemed an almost silly word to use. But that was what Gerard was—the man with whom she was having a relationship. Her boyfriend. She looked at him striding down the beach beside Jake, two men with a purpose. She wondered what they were talking about. Was Gerard confiding in Jake about his relationship with her?

Helen wanted to talk about their relationship with someone, but she wasn't at all convinced Grace was the person with whom she should share her thoughts. Better to wait and call Sylvia. But Helen couldn't help herself. She reacted to her thoughts, a very old, ineffective habit.

"What are you thinking?" she asked Grace, who had been trudging along beside her. Helen initiated the conversation like a crab walking sideways, hoping Grace might ask her what was on her mind.

"I was thinking about hot chocolate with whipped cream. And grilled cheese sandwiches with tomato soup."

"Are you hungry?"

"Always. Ever since I started nursing."

"Well, you do need to make up for the extra calories," Helen said, aware that her own thoughts were flying around in her head like gnats.

"That's what the midwives told me. But I have also put on ten pounds."

"It's all in your boobs."

"Thanks, Mom."

"That's not a criticism, Gracie. It's a fact. Do you want to turn around now and go get something to eat?"

"No, I'm fine. The fresh air will do Frankie good. Me too."

They walked on in silence, with Helen still anxious to discuss her situation. But she accepted her place as a mother, a grandmother, might just be to offer support, to listen and console. Her days of being the one with issues and needs were gone. It was her time to offer encouragement, not to seek it. For Helen, whose self-centeredness had not completely disappeared—nor would it ever—this was an uncomfortable truth.

As if reading her mother's mind, Grace interrupted. "So, I never really said I think it's great. Gerard is a great guy."

"He is."

"Then what is it, Mom?"

"What do you mean?"

"You don't seem as happy as I would expect you to be. New man. Nice man. New life."

Helen couldn't stop herself from blurting out, "It's just that it is all so complicated. How will we manage our houses, our jobs, our families?"

Grace looked surprised. "Gerard has a family? I thought his parents were both dead, and he was an only child."

"Well, my family then. Our family. What if he wants to live in Wales? How could I miss Frankie's growing up?"

Grace was silent for a moment, telling Helen the thought had already crossed her mind. "That's a hard one. I would hate that. But there are planes and vacations. Skype. Texts. It could work."

"It wouldn't be the same."

"The same as what? We have never done this before."

Helen grew silent. She was embarrassed to tell Grace the truth, and the truth was she was afraid if she went to live in Wales, Grace would become more attached to Jake's family, who only lived in New York City. Helen imagined Grace's little family spending every holiday with them—the poet and the teacher—and having Frankie grow up believing she had only one real set of grandparents, not two. She and Gerard would be those absentee grandparents who sent toys and money but had no impact on their grandchild's life.

"Wow!" Grace cut in. "Whatever you are thinking, your face just fell into all kinds of serious."

"It's nothing!" Helen replied brightly.

"Tell your eyes that. You are crying."

"It's just the wind," Helen said, wiping away the tears and blowing her nose on a tissue she had retrieved from her pocket.

"I'm just going to say this one time, Mom." Helen braced herself for what she imagined might be coming. "You have a right to be happy. You have a responsibility to be happy. The Universe wants you to be happy."

Helen reached out and took Grace's mittened hand in her own. "Thank you, sweetie. I want to be happy."

"I want you to be happy too, Mom."

They continued on their trek down the beach. The men, deep in conversation, had reached the impassable inlet and turned back, walking toward Helen and Grace.

"Jake really likes Gerard," Grace commented. "You know what's funny? They are almost the same age."

"Really?" Helen exclaimed, not exactly sure how that made her feel.

"Jake is thirty-five. He's eight years older than I am. And Gerard, he's forty-two, right?"

Helen nodded.

"I think that's why they get along so well. And other things."

"I am glad they do."

"You know, Mom, no matter where you two end up, we will always make time to be with you. Jake loves you. Frankie loves you. I love you, and most of all, I will always need my mom."

Helen was touched by her daughter's sentiment and began to cry again. "Thanks for that, darling. It means a lot to me," she said, wiping away her tears.

"Wind?"

Helen laughed. "Wind."

"Now, what did you want to talk about, Mom?"

Helen reached over and pulled her daughter close in a hug, kissing her forehead. "Nothing. Nothing at all. Let's go make cocoa."

Gerard wanted to "nap" with Helen. The cold air and bracing wind had already sent Grace and Frankie to lie down. It was only Jake, who sat on the plush sofa in front of the fire, drinking a beer, who stood between Gerard's lust and Helen's self-consciousness.

As Helen fussed in the kitchen, wiping counters and putting away pots and pans, Gerard turned to Jake. "She's nervous. She doesn't know how to be a mother and a lover at the same time."

"Women. They sure do complicate the hell out of everything." Jake took a long swig of his beer.

"They certainly do." Gerard smiled, lifting his bottle to clink against Jake's and taking a long swig himself.

"What are you two celebrating?" Helen called from the kitchen.

"Nothing!" they replied in unison, then broke into laughter.

"Seriously, dude," Jake said, "you should go get her. I'll watch the fire, and I promise, I won't give you two a second thought." He winked at Gerard. "I'll put my earphones on and listen to an Alan Watts podcast. Good for an hour. Now, go."

Gerard rose and went to the kitchen, empty bottle in hand. He put the bottle in the recycling bin and then stood behind Helen, who was trying to erase the flecks in the granite countertop. He pushed her hair to one side and nuzzled her neck, nibbling her soft flesh lightly, which sent goosebumps all over her body. She shivered.

"Cold?" he asked.

"You know I'm not."

"Shall I continue?"

"It's so—"

"Complicated?" he said, finishing her sentence for her. "Only, it is not. Grace and Frankie are sleeping. Jake is zoning out in front of the fire with a beer and a podcast. We have a good forty-five minutes to spend together if we hurry."

Helen looked up from her cleaning, concern on her face. "What if …." Gerard tipped her face up toward his and kissed her deeply. "All right. Let's go."

As Gerard undressed her, he kissed her tenderly on her wrists, her inner arms, her nipples, her thighs. Helen felt the old tug pull her from really enjoying what was going on. Here was a handsome man, nineteen years her junior, who evidently thought she was the cat's pajamas. But why? What could he possibly see in her? She was sixty-one, wrinkled, flabby.

"Helen," Gerard's voice brought her back abruptly. "Are you thinking again?"

"You know I am."

"Well, stop thinking and pay attention to this." He pressed her shoulders down so she was kneeling in front of him. He drew her head gently closer to him, encouraging her to take all of him in her mouth.

When she did, and she began to tease him with her tongue, she felt him respond, which encouraged her even more. She forgot the inhibitions she had brought with her into the room. No longer was she sixty-one and he forty-two. She was a sexual woman who enjoyed feasting on her lover's lust. It excited her as much as she felt it exciting him. He pulled out quickly, helped her up to lean over the bed, and entered her. As he thrust himself into her repeatedly, she could feel her desire mounting until, suddenly, in a single, shuddering burst, they came together. Then, he lay on top of her, muttering "Oh, my God" over and over again.

Helen was pleased. Her former husband had never been enthusiastic about sex, never made her feel she was desirable. Now, if she could just let go of the inhibitions she carried with her, she was sure she and Gerard would enjoy a long and lusty life.

But of course, she reminded herself, *that's not all he loves about me.*

Gerard stood up and looked at his watch. "Twenty-two minutes to spare. Shall we go again?"

Helen laughed to herself. *Maybe it is.*

That evening after a dinner of lamb stew and baby greens, followed by a warm apple crisp topped with ice cream, they all settled down in front of the fire to watch one of Helen's favorite movies, *Love, Actually*. Gracie's favorite too. They had watched this movie together every holiday since Grace was old enough to appreciate the "porn" scenes for what they were—not porn, but a sweet, if ironic, way to bring a couple of young people together.

Helen loved the movie for its rich texture of relationships. The Alan Rifkin character and his sleezy assistant with whom he had an affair reminded her of her ex-husband Frank. But Helen no longer wept like Emma Thompson over the demise of her marriage. She had found something far more satisfying in her relationship with Gerard. He was helping her, allowing her to break through some of the chains that held her—control, insecurity, fear. His love for her was so genuine and boundless. How could she have ever thought she could just walk away?

When Keira Knightley walked down the aisle with her new husband, and the trumpets blasted "Love, love, love," Helen turned to Gerard.

"That's not exactly what I want our wedding to be," she whispered to him, "but something along those lines."

"I'll see what I can do," he replied, giving her hand a squeeze. He was thinking of the Men's Welsh Choir he sang with back home, and a lovely castle with enough nooks and crannies to hold musicians with bagpipes.

Helen panicked. Had she inadvertently mentioned the "M" word? She turned to Gerard. "I didn't mean that …."

"Yes, you did. And I love you for it all the more. Now, settle down and stop being ridiculous."

Grace sat mesmerized, chomping on caramel popcorn while the lobsters attended the nativity, and Prime Minister Hugh Grant danced down the stairs and across the floors of 10 Downing Street in his underwear. Love, love, love was in the air, and everyone, even Frankie, who cooperated wonderfully by sleeping and nursing through the whole movie, was taken in by the film's humor and its message.

As if on cue, when the credits rolled, the phone rang. It was Jake's parents calling to wish everyone a Happy New Year. They were in Belize on vacation, returning the following day as Jake's father had to go back to school.

"How's the weather?" Jake asked, not really caring but knowing they would want to brag just a little, as if they had personally created the flawless skies and crystal-clear water.

"It's been glorious. Not a hint of rain during the day, and raucous storms at night," cooed Jake's mother, the poet. "I've done a lot of writing. This place is so inspirational."

"Good for you, Mom. What did Dad do while you were working?"

"Not working, Jake. *Being*. I am *being* here, *being* inspired."

"So, what did Dad do while you were busy *being inspired*?"

"Not busy, Jake—"

"Mom! Dad?"

"Oh, he was with his buddies."

"Dad has buddies there?"

"You know—Michael Connelly, Lee Childs, David Baldacci."

"Oh, *those* friends." Jake smiled. He and Grace had given him an early Christmas gift of the latest releases. Jake was glad to know he had brought them along.

"How's the baby? Grace?"

"Great. Everyone's great. Helen and Gerard are going steady."

"Who?"

"Helen, Grace's mother, Mom."

"I know that, but who is the fellow?"

"Gerard. He's from Wales. He has been on sabbatical at Yale."

"That was quick."

"Mom," Jake said roughly.

"I don't suppose we will be invited."

"Invited?"

"To the wedding."

"I don't know, Mom, a wedding may be a long time coming."

"I guess at our age, you don't want to wait too long."

Jake was going to mention Gerard was almost the same age as he, but he thought better of it. He didn't want to prolong the conversation.

"So, we will see you soon?" he asked.

"That's just it. We would like to visit this coming weekend, if that works."

"I will check with Grace. That should be fine, but she is in bed now, and I will have to talk to her tomorrow. Enjoy the rest of your trip! Love to Dad."

"Love to you too, sweetheart."

Jake hung up with a sigh.

"Your mother?" Grace asked when he put the phone down. Jake nodded. "I am in bed? You lied to your mother?"

"I embellished the truth. You are in your pajamas."

"Why did you feel the need to lie to your mother?" Grace prodded. Helen and Gerard looked on in amusement, though Helen was eager to hear his reply.

"Haven't you ever lied to your mother?" Jake exclaimed. That was not the response Helen had expected. Grace looked over at her mother, whose expression had changed from one of amusement to concern. "Be honest now, Grace," Jake chided.

After a pause, Grace spoke. "Well, I suppose once or twice. But only to save your feelings, Mom. Not over anything big."

"Like your wedding?" Helen still felt she had been slighted, cheated even from enjoying her only child's nuptials.

"You are not still upset about that, are you? It has been over a year!" Grace cried.

"Relax, darling. I never was upset over that. Really, I felt it was more my fault than yours."

"I tell you what," Jake said, putting his hand on Grace's shoulder, "let's not go there. Let's keep this the lovely evening that it was until my mother called."

"What did she want anyway?" Grace asked as she rocked a fussing Frankie in her arms.

"Nothing. Just Happy New Year, and they want to come visit us this coming weekend."

"Well, they can't stay with us. There is no room," Grace asserted.

"They could stay here," Helen offered. "I have plenty of room. It will be nice to get to know them a little better."

"And I will be gone," Gerard added. Just then, the sonorous bells of the grandfather clock chimed out the hour. Helen felt each of the gongs strike her, a sword through her heart. Gerard was going home. Back to Wales. She wouldn't see him for months, unless, of course, she made the trek across the Atlantic over spring break. Maybe this was all a mistake, a childish fantasy. Wouldn't it be easier to just be a widow and live out her life alone? Did she really want all this disruption? Was it love she felt or mere attraction, a break in the boredom of her life?

She looked over at Gerard, who was now holding the baby in his arms. He was humming something to her, some Welsh thing no doubt, and both he and the baby looked peaceful and serene. How he could go from being a lion in bed, gently biting her shoulder as he thrust himself into her, to this gentle man, so loving and serene, was beyond her. Well, before it wasn't beyond her, exactly; it intrigued her. Gerard had caught her attention and held it. She liked that. She liked his complexity, his ability to surprise her. Like when he said he loved her for her mind. Who would have thought, as good as they were at sex with one another, he would have chosen that? She didn't choose that. She was first and foremost attracted to the way he looked and then to what he thought. Now, of course, the two elements had blended together, and she loved all of him, she believed, because of who he was and who she had come to know over the past months. Now would come the true test of their relationship. Could they maintain their love for each other more than 3,000 miles away?

Gerard knew Helen well enough to know this was just what she was thinking. "It is going to be all right, you know. Soldiers have been doing this with their sweethearts for centuries. And all over the world, couples are separated by their jobs—"

"Stop!" Helen cried. "You don't need to convince me. I am fully aware of the cost of being in a long-distance relationship."

"Mom! You don't need to be so mean. Gerard is just trying to—"

"Gracie," Jake said, squeezing his wife's shoulder, "don't you think it is time we put Frankie down for the night? And then turn in ourselves? We have got to be up early. Back to the grind."

Grace rose, retrieving Frankie from Gerard's arms, and went over to her mother. She kissed Helen on the cheek, then whispered in her ear, "I'm sorry, Mom, I didn't mean to bark. It's just that you've got a keeper. Don't let this one get away." Then Grace turned to Gerard. "It has been great seeing you, Gerard. You are one of the good ones." Her words were met with his generous, sincere smile.

Helen and Gerard watched the little family pad off around the corner and to bed.

❈

In the living room, the last of the logs on the fire crackled and split, shooting sparks of glowing red onto the floor of the hearth.

"How are we going to do this?" Helen asked at last.

"Just as we have been doing it all along. Only, you will work here, and I will work there. We will see each other on the holidays. In the meanwhile, we can use Skype or FaceTime or whatever you like to video chat."

"What if this COVID threat develops into something bigger?"

"We will deal with that bridge when we have to cross it," Gerard replied reasonably.

He took her face in his hands and pulled her toward him. She closed her eyes, and he kissed each of her lids, lightly, and then her mouth, with more passion. Helen readjusted herself on the couch, less to be coy than her ankle was stinging her, but Gerard took her cozying up to him and tucking herself into his shoulder as a very positive sign.

"I can't give up my daughter, my granddaughter, this place."

"I am not asking you to."

"But I would be so selfish to ask you to give up your home in Wales."

"I am not intending to," Gerard stated matter-of-factly.

Helen was confused. Ever since Gerard had placed the gold bracelet on her wrist, she had ruminated over the options available. Either she moved to Wales or he moved here. There was no in-between. Or was there?

"What do you mean?" she asked.

"Why can't we have it all?" he replied.

This thought had not occurred to Helen who *had* had it all once—the marriage, the job, the house, the status, the cars. Then she watched them all come tumbling down. Now she was leery; was having it all too high an expectation, was it being too greedy in a Universe where so many had nothing at all? She felt as if she were being asked to choose—an impossible choice, really—between the comfortable life she now enjoyed in her little house, with Grace and Jake and Frankie close by, rounding out the years in the job she had been at for decades, cruising toward the end.

And then there was Plan B with Gerard. Move to Wales. Let go of all attachments and follow her heart. Learn new things. Be in a new place where every day would be an adventure. Was she too old for adventure? For the stimulation she would feel every day as she found new images to feed her soul. She could discover new ways to cook and talk and spell. A whole new language! It would be exhilarating and exhausting, but at the end of the day, she would come home to Gerard. He would exhilarate her more. She was exhausted just thinking about it.

Helen rose from the couch.

"Where are you going?" Gerard asked.

"I need some wine. You want something?"

"I'll take a beer."

In the kitchen, Helen turned on the tulip-shaped lamps that hung over the yellow counter. The room was bathed in gold. *Maybe we can have it all*, she thought as she poured some pale chardonnay into her goblet. Maybe it was time for her to let go of her limited thinking and embrace all the Universe had to offer. She didn't know, but she knew who would.

"Well?" Gerard asked her as he took the cold beer from her hand.

She looked at him and saw both expectation and desire in his green eyes. She felt her own desire well up inside her.

"What do you want to do?" he asked, not pushing.

The answer came quickly and firmly. "I want to call Sylvia."

Sylvia did better than just to talk to Helen. She invited Helen down to visit her at her rental home in North Carolina for a few days, to clear her head before returning to Yale for winter term. Helen had first met Sylvia a year before when she and Grace had checked in to Sylvia's place for Christmas. Helen was still reeling from the devastating blow her ex-husband Frank, now deceased, had dealt her by running off with his assistant. At the time, Helen thought the solution to her anguish lay in looking up old beaus, rekindling old flames. It turned out, though, that her old boyfriend Micah, who ran an antiques business outside of Charlotte, had a new flame of his own. A younger man, accomplished in many areas. The couple, now married, had moved to Connecticut, not far from Helen's home. Was there irony in this? Helen certainly grimaced at the humor.

"So what do you say, pet?" Sylvia chirped into the phone. "You say your young man is leaving for Wales tomorrow. Why not just catch a flight down here? You can stay for a few days, relax here. My treat."

Helen considered Sylvia's offer. It would be a good thing to get away for a bit. The change of scene would ease the sting of Gerard's departure. Certainly, time spent with Sylvia could have nothing but a good effect. Suddenly, she remembered she had planned to invite Jake's parents to the house for the weekend. A thought crossed Helen's mind, a new thought for her: *Why don't I ask everyone about this plan and how it affects them?* She had gone too many years making decisions on her own without consulting Frank or Grace or anyone, just justifying her arrangements by convincing herself that somehow, she was so important, she could simply ignore other people's needs. Look where that had gotten her. But now, with Gerard, with Grace and Jake and Frankie, and with Sylvia too, she had another chance. She could, of course, make the same mistake, but now she was determined to do just the opposite.

Once she had hung up from her conversation with Sylvia, promising a return call in the morning, she climbed the stairs to her bedroom, flicking off lights along the way. She arrived at her room where Gerard was waiting for her in bed.

"Everything all right?" he asked, looking over his reading glasses. He was reading the latest mystery novel by C. J. Box, an American writer who intrigued him with his take on the West. This was Jake's present to Gerard, whom he knew was a fan. "This fellow, by the way, is bloody excellent. His books just keep getting better and better."

Helen was in the bathroom, brushing her teeth. "Can't hear you," she mumbled, her mouth full of toothpaste. When she emerged, wearing white silk pajamas and her flowered kimono robe, her copper hair curling over her shoulders, Gerard took in a deep breath.

"A vision. You are a vision. I can't possibly leave you," Gerard said, putting his book down and patting the bed beside him. Helen didn't move. "What is it, Helen? Have I … ?"

"It's nothing, not you anyway. Sylvia wants me to go spend a few days with her before school. Fly out tomorrow."

"Sounds lovely. What is the problem?"

"I told Jake and Grace that his parents could stay here for the weekend."

"Yes?"

"I will be gone. And there is the dog." As if on cue, Perdita, Helen's apricot-colored mongrel, jumped up on the bed.

"So, let them stay here. Grace and Jake can stay in the guest room. The parents can have your bed. They can drink all your booze, throw a wild party as long as they clean up. What do you care?"

Helen smiled at Gerard, stroking his cheek. "You are so wonderful. You cut through everything. But won't they think me rude?"

"Why rude? They don't really want to see you, now, do they? It's Frankie they want to see. Quality time with their grandchild. Their son. Now, come to bed. Let's see if there isn't something I can do to wipe that worry off your face."

Helen giggled as Gerard pulled her under the covers. "Oh, my!"

Chapter 3

January 2, 2020

The next morning, when Helen spoke to Grace, presenting the same dilemma, Grace's response was just as Gerard's had been.

"That's perfect, Mom! Thank you so much! And as for your trip down to see Sylvia, don't worry, we'll take care of Perdita while you are gone, and we won't drink too much of your wine."

Helen felt both relieved and confused. She was glad she had sought help with her dilemma, and they had all concurred with her plan. Now, she looked forward to getting away and doing something for herself, but she was confused as to why it was always so damned hard to go through with it. Why did there always have to be a committee in her head, questioning her decisions, saddling her with guilt, leaping to negative consequences? Three days away, two nights. It wasn't like she was going around the world.

Helen, she told herself with a sigh, *you think too much*. But wasn't it her brain that had gotten her where she was—top of her field, sought after for her expertise? There was that, but, too, there was the exhausting battle that took place in her head always.

Maybe I should see a therapist. She had done that, and it had done no good. How could Gerard possibly love her for her mind? It felt so bruised and damaged. How could she erase these negative thoughts and emotions that populated her head? Grace had said, If you have a question, and you put it out to the Universe, it will be answered. But what if someone didn't trust the Universe to come through? What if the Universe felt hostile and unforgiving?

Helen realized as soon as she thought those words that they were bullshit. The Universe had been treating her great all the way along. All the blessings she had been given—Grace, Frankie, Gerard, her job, her home, her health—even the sorrows with her parents, her divorce, and Webb, her first love who had killed himself the year before, these were all necessary parts of the life she was leading now. There was nothing to be but grateful. So why did she feel the bottom would drop out any minute? Why did she find herself sounding brittle, as if she were made of porcelain, about to break? Why was she always looking to do the perfect thing, as if she knew what that was? She was trapped halfway in a glass half empty. She was a prisoner of her mind. *Universe,* she prayed silently, *I don't want to fuck this up. Please help me.* She said it from the bottom of her heart, hoping an understanding and loving Creator would hear her.

Chapter 4

They were booked on evening flights, so Helen spent the next day doing laundry and cleaning up around the house, changing sheets on the beds, polishing the baths, and making sure there were ample towels and toilet paper for everyone. She emptied the fridge and scrubbed the shelves until they shone, discarding the leftovers and leaving an almost minimalist collection of a box of eggs, six Fiji waters, two red peppers, and some brie cheese. And, of course, a few bottles of wine. She vacuumed, dusted, sprayed, and sponged until Gerard, choking on the fumes, asked, "Do they really require all this sterilization? Or is it just you being anxious?"

Helen swiped at some stray strands of auburn hair from her forehead with hands concealed in yellow rubber gloves. "I don't know why," she said, "but I am a little anxious."

"About what?" Gerard asked as he wrapped his arms around her.

"I don't know," Helen said, swallowing a sob that was rising dangerously in her throat. "You leaving. Both of us getting on planes. Seeing Sylvia again."

Gerard led her over to the sofa. "Come sit," he said, patting the soft couch. As she did, she peeled off the glove so she could hold his hand. "First of all, you know the statistics about flying."

"I know. Safest way to travel. It's not the physics of travel that bothers me, it's the distance that it will put between us."

"Helen, look at me." Gerard lifted her chin, gently turning her face toward his. "Just because the lights are out, does that mean power no longer exists?"

"Of course not."

"Well, the same is true of my love for you. Just because we're not together physically, doesn't mean I won't be present with you every minute."

Helen thought about this for a minute. It was a lovely sentiment but impractical. What about *out of sight, out of mind*? Honestly, it wasn't Gerard she was worried about, it was herself. She had a particular ability to focus solely on tasks at hand, to forget those who were not with her, to immerse herself in her own world at the expense of relationships. While she did not want this to happen, she was afraid she would be powerless against her old behavior.

"But what if something happens? What if—"

Gerard put a finger over her lips to keep her from talking. "Sometimes, you are a difficult woman to love, Helen Ferry. You know as well as I do that 'things' happen all the time, and there's not a damned thing we can do about it except accept and adapt. Have a little faith that everything is going to work out. And better than you expect."

"You are right," Helen concurred. "I'm sure everything will be fine." Though in her heart, she harbored doubt and felt slightly bruised by his comments, which seemed to border on a scolding.

"Feel better? Still anxious?"

"Well, there is Sylvia. I'm nervous about seeing her," she said, moving on from her own insecurities.

Gerard looked confused. "Why? Isn't she your best supporter, your greatest friend?"

"More like my Yoda. My Zen Master."

"And you are afraid she is going to give you some impossible task, like drinking the ocean up through a straw or tipping a mountain with your nose."

Helen giggled at the thought of Sylvia making such demands.

"Not that exactly but along those lines. She's bound to ask me to change."

"So, why are you going?"

"Because I value her opinion. I need her advice. And I want the distraction when you leave."

"So, what is the problem?" Gerard asked gently.

"There is none, really."

"So, what is the problem?" Gerard repeated.

"Who is the Zen Master now?" Helen laughed.

Gerard moved a long strand of hair that had fallen onto Helen's cheek.

"Helen, Helen, Helen," he murmured.

"I know. I am a complete bitch."

"Complicated, yes. Bitch, perhaps. Human, most definitely. As are we all."

Helen lay her head back on the couch with her eyes closed, holding Gerard's warm hand and feeling, for the moment, that everything was all right.

Later, as they packed their suitcases, Helen wondered what it would be like to pack for Wales, to have this steady relationship turn into something more serious, something she could really commit to and grasp tightly. But maybe that was the whole point. Maybe she had to stop grasping for Love. She needed to let this story fold and unfold, like a piece of blank paper transformed into an origami swan. So much better when it was allowed to be true to its purpose, whatever that was.

Helen folded enough panties for four days at Sylvia's, plus an extra in case of accidents. She wasn't getting any younger, and leaks were not an uncommon thing. How Gerard could find her appealing when she found herself so flawed was beyond her. *But it's my mind*, she reminded herself, *he loves me for my mind*. Though, his kisses told a different tale. She brought several lightweight shirts and some heavier ones as well—the weather in North Carolina was unpredictable. Jeans, both black and blue, two sweaters and pajamas, socks, bras, a robe. Her case swelled when she zipped it shut.

"Wow!" Gerard exclaimed, astonished. "How long are you going for?"

"A woman needs her things," was Helen's curt reply.

Gerard picked up his little satchel, which looked like it couldn't carry more than a laptop. It held all he had brought for his brief visit.

"Show off," Helen said, sticking out her tongue.

"Be careful. That's a dangerous invitation. Anyway, I like to travel light."

"Well, I am a girl," Helen replied.

"You certainly are."

Helen stuck her tongue out again. Gerard put his bag down and started to move toward her. "I warned you not to stick that thing out unless you are prepared for the consequences." The consequences were just what Helen was hoping for.

Later that evening, Gracie, Jake, and Frankie arrived to give them a lift to the airport. Helen was glad for the opportunity to hold her granddaughter close once more. Despite what Gerard had told her about the safety of the flights, and the security of her home, Helen felt a rumbling anxiety. Maybe she was just hungry? She had fed Gerard a cheddar and turkey sandwich at noon but neglected to fix anything for herself.

She went to the kitchen, cut a piece of banana bread, and put it in the microwave. Then, sharing her piece with Perdita, the little apricot mophead standing at her feet, she turned to Grace. "You will be very good to her," Helen said.

Grace, who was nursing the baby, did not even look up. "Yes, I'll be very good to her."

"Feel free to spoil her."

"Haven't you done that already?"

"Yes, I suppose I have," Helen said as she leaned over and picked Perdita up in her arms. "She gets lonely. She will want to sleep with you. And she will need you to take her out, even in the snow, or she will pee on the sofa."

"Charming. Got it. Do you want us to take her to the movies with us?"

"Very funny. Just please keep her safe."

"I know how much you love her, Mom. I will take good care of her." Helen fed Perdita the last bite of her banana bread. She wished it were as easy as that.

All the way to the airport, Gerard held Helen's hand. They insisted on sitting in the back with Frankie in her car seat. Gracie and Jake were in front. Helen's anxiety kept mounting, rearing up every once in a while, like a wild stallion pounding its hooves against her chest. Then, she would blow out a little air, and Gerard would squeeze her hand tightly. For the moment, the worry was gone. She was here, now, with the people she most loved in the world. Surely, the Universe would keep them safe. Surely, God would protect them. She told herself to relax.

Grace turned on the radio. It was Queen, ever so popular since the release of *Bohemian Rhapsody*. Only this song, "We Will Rock You," had been made memorable by *A Knight's Tale*, with that sweet, young Australian actor who had accidentally overdosed. Heath Ledger. Why should anyone so young, so handsome, so talented and successful die?

Helen didn't want to think about life and death. She didn't know what she wanted to think about. She didn't want to think at all.

"So, I'm sure your parents can't wait to see Frankie again, Jake. I'm sorry, what are their names again?" Helen asked, breaking the silence.

"Liz and Richard."

Helen started laughing.

"Ma-ah-ahm," Gracie whined, turning a one-syllable word into a three-syllable rant.

"Liz and Richard. I just realized. You know—Elizabeth Taylor and Richard Burton," Helen laughed lightly.

"They get that a lot," Jake said, smiling. "I think they got married just for that."

"Jake!" Grace cried.

"What? Just saying."

Helen joined back in the conversation. "Names are a curious thing. Did you know that being named Helen has shaped many relationships in my life?"

"Really?" Jake said, playing along. "How?"

"Well, people always associate me with Helen of Troy."

Gerard brought Helen's hand to his lips. "The face that launched a thousand ships."

"Oh, please," Grace muttered under her breath.

"Exactly. Or Heloise and Abelard," Helen continued.

"That's more like Eloise, Mom. No fair. What about me? Try being named Constance Grace."

"Dude, that's heavy. How did I not know that? Constance? Like Constant? Constant Grace? Whoa, that's heavy," Jake mocked his wife.

"Dude! Eyes on the road!" Grace jabbed him in the side with her elbow.

"C'mon. Lighten up. A name's a name," Jake said.

"Until it takes on a life of its own. My name has enough baggage to fill a roll-on cart at the Plaza," Grace asserted.

"You will never forgive me, will you?" Helen asked.

"Tell you what. Let's just call you Jennifer and have done with it. Only, we will spell it with one 'n' so you'll still be special," Jake offered. "Of course, then we will be Jake and Jen, slightly echoing—"

"You, be quiet! I was saying I am just teasing. I love my name. I didn't used to, but now, like I have said before, it is not so much a name as a way of life."

"I approve," Gerard piped up from the back seat. "Grace as a way of life. We could all benefit from that."

Helen leaned back in her seat. That was the truth, wasn't it? If she believed, really believed, in Grace, God's grace, then there was no need to worry. Whatever happened was going to be all right. She sighed, closing her eyes, and leaned against Gerard's shoulder as she dozed off to sleep.

What seemed like only minutes later, the sound of the blinker woke her. The car turned, bringing her and Gerard closer. She opened her eyes. They had arrived at the airport, and exchanged quick kisses all around as the place was bustling, even at this time of the evening.

She sent Gerard off to his gate, managing not to spill any tears, while she bustled off in the opposite direction toward hers. But not before they exchanged a lingering kiss and a promise to keep in touch, to remember she was his girl, and to reaffirm their love for one another one last time. Helen could practically hear Gracie shouting, "Get a room!" She gave Gerard one last kiss and walked away, feeling the gray ache in her stomach that came whenever she had to say goodbye. Maybe Sylvia could help her with that. She hoped Sylvia would help her with many things.

Helen was not at all surprised when Sylvia greeted her wearing the same Christmas tree flannel pajamas and sheepskin slippers she had been wearing a year ago when Helen and Grace had stayed at the rental home for the first time. Helen felt as if time had stopped, and in some ways, she wished it had.

"Don't just stand there brooding. Come in! Get out of the cold!" Sylvia said, taking Helen's arm. "How was the trip?"

Helen grimaced. "Oh, you know. Planes. Airports. Charlotte traffic."

"Notoriously bad," Sylvia concurred. "But now you are here. Safely in one piece. Let's take your bag down to your room." As Helen followed Sylvia down the hall, she noticed the old woman limping and, every once in a while, drawing in a breath.

"Are you all right, Sylvia? Did you have a fall?" Helen asked, genuinely concerned.

"It's nothing," Sylvia responded. "Nothing but time. Let's go have a cup of decaf tea, shall we, before bed. Or would you like something stronger?"

"Tea would be perfect," Helen replied, immediately regretting her response. In truth, she would really have liked two shots of whiskey and a warm bed. Enough to dull the mischief in her brain.

While Sylvia filled the electric kettle and took down a box of herbal tea from the cupboard, Helen looked around the house. Cozy as ever, it brought back pleasant memories.

The house still smelled of cinnamon and rich roll cookies. The tree still stood in the corner, the star just touching the ceiling, branches shimmering with tinsel and tiny lights. Helen felt herself ease into the magic of the moment. She was glad she had come.

As they waited for the kettle to boil, Sylvia filled a plate with cookies. "So, tell me, pet, what brings you all the way down here? Not that I am not delighted, but it is a long way to come for a cup of tea."

Helen sat down on the couch in front of the fire which, though on its way out for the evening, still glowed red with tiny flames spiking every now and then. She took a long breath in through her nostrils, held it, and then let out a long sigh, grateful for this practice yoga had taught her.

"It's Gerard."

"Your Welshman."

"He has asked me to go steady." Sylvia laughed, almost spitting out her tea.

"Good gracious! Aren't you both a little old for that?"

"My thought exactly."

"You mean thoughts?" Sylvia said, nibbling the corners off a cookie.

Helen nodded, lifting the tea cup to her lips. Before she had even taken a sip, she put the cup down. "You know, Syl, I think I will take that whiskey now."

"Help yourself," Sylvia said, motioning with her hand toward the cupboard where she kept the booze, though Helen remembered quite well from last time. "Do you love him? Does he love you?"

"Yes. I think so."

"Not good enough, pet. Either you really love him, or you just need him. You love the idea of him."

Helen sipped on her whiskey. She didn't really need Gerard. If anything, he was an inconvenience living so far away. She had her beach house she loved. She had her daughter and her granddaughter nearby. She had her job, good for another decade if she wished.

"So, how can you possibly jeopardize all that … and with a long-distance relationship?" Sylvia interjected quietly.

"Was I saying that out loud?"

Sylvia nodded.

"I have a habit of doing that, sober or drunk."

"One of your endearing qualities, Helen. It is called transparency. Don't ever lose it." The old woman patted Helen's hand, then passed her the plate of cookies. "Try one."

Helen could not resist. The rich, warm smell of vanilla emanated from the cookies that had been cut in many holiday shapes and decorated with frosting and sprinkles. "I'll have a bell," Helen giggled.

"A wise choice," Sylvia smiled. "Second only to a star."

They sat on the sofa, munching on cookies. Helen sipped her drink, and the fire sparkled in her eyes.

"You make all this so bearable, so fun," Helen said, breaking the silence. "It reminds me of when Grace was little, and I wasn't so consumed by my work. Those Christmases, Frank would pile us all into the station wagon, and we would drive off to find a pine tree to chop down. Those were days of sugar cookies and monkey bread, whipped cream moustaches and snowball fights. It was a magical time."

Sylvia nodded her head in agreement, sipping on her tea and helping herself to a sugar angel frosted in white and silver.

"But then it changed," Helen continued. "I became something of a celebrity. No more pine trees. We just dragged the artificial one out of its box in the attic. No more cookies. No more time for baking, and anyway, everyone I knew was gluten-free. Christmas became more about the presents, the money spent on each other to prove how much we loved, rather than the time spent together to show we really did care." Helen took a breath from her diatribe to take another swig of her drink. "I want the old Christmas back. I want this magic back." Even as she said it, she knew that ship had sailed long ago. Frank was dead. Grace had a family of her own. This was the part she hated about life—it never stood still.

"Is Gerard an impediment to that?"

Thoughts circled in Helen's mind. *An impediment?* These past two weeks with him had been lovely, both in Wales and at her home. There had been merrymaking, lovemaking, cookie baking. Grace had been there with Frankie, and it had all been great fun. But then, like an atom exploding, everyone set off back into their own corners of the Universe.

She remembered as a child being put in a dark closet for punishment. Five minutes in there had seemed like an eternity. She had dreaded that feeling ever since. Loneliness was such a random thing. She could feel lonely in a crowded room. Just as she could feel content if she were absorbed, all alone, in her writing. The loneliness she felt now, of not belonging to anyone, with anyone, was almost more than she could bear.

"You think too much, pet," Sylvia said. "Enough of this tea. Go pour me some whiskey, will you? I have a feeling it is going to be a long night. And put another log on the fire while you are at it. There's a dear."

"How do you do it?" Helen asked as she gave Sylvia her drink and refilled her own. "How do you manage to maintain such cheerfulness when you are all alone?"

"That's just it. I am never alone. I stay in the present moment, and I find that I am complete as I bake, and sing, and feed my birds. I talk to the firewood and thank it for giving me warmth. I talk to the bubbles in my bath and thank them for healing my aching bones. I talk to the Universe and thank it for bringing me this far, for giving me such a wonderful life. I am present in my day, and every day becomes a present."

Helen looked skeptical. "It's hard to be present when you are not. I would be living 1,000 miles away from my home, my family, if I were to move to Wales."

"Longer. It is definitely longer than 1,000 miles."

"Whatever."

"Why can't he move to America?"

Helen was genuinely shocked by the suggestion, not that the thought hadn't occurred to her already. "I couldn't do that! That is so much to ask! I would feel so selfish."

Sylvia rose and walked over to the Christmas tree. She rearranged several of the ornaments so the lights sparkled more profusely. Then, she turned to Helen. "I want you to listen to what I am saying, pet, without critiquing what I am saying. Listen with an open heart and mind. Can you do that?"

"That is why I am here," Helen whispered.

"Good. You love Gerard, you say, but how well do you even know him? Do you love him just enough to be able to live without him, or do you love him so much that you can't imagine life in his absence?"

Helen sat quietly, her hands in her lap. After a few moments, Sylvia prodded her for an answer. "Go on then. Answer the question."

"You told me to listen."

"Helen. Really."

"All right then. The truth?"

"The truth."

"I'm not sure. I have gotten so used to living on my own that I don't feel like I need someone in my life. I love Gerard, but really, do I need Gerard?"

"And yet, you need him to ask you to marry him."

"How did you know that?" Helen asked, astonished.

"I have my sources," Sylvia smiled. "This is not King Lear—'reason not the need.' This is real life. He is a real man with real feelings for you. So, do you want him in your life? Is your life better with him in it?"

"Oh, yes," Helen replied enthusiastically, in part because she was worried Sylvia might think she was just using Gerard. Which she wasn't. "I adore being with him. He makes me feel so alive, so young, so happy."

"But ..." Sylvia noticed a pall starting to cover Helen's face.

"But I have been so selfish all my life. With Frank. With Grace. I can't do this to Grace again, shut her out. And Gerard ... I can't ask him to leave his home."

Sylvia took Helen's hands in her own. "You know, all these people are adults. They can make their own choices. You don't owe anyone anything. "

"That's not true!"

"But it is. Frankie is going to grow up with a mother and father who love her. If Grandma is always there, getting in the way, how is that going to make them feel?"

"But I can help them."

"Of course you can, without becoming one of those helicopter grandparents who hover over their grandchildren like a hawk. They need breathing space. And you do too. A grandmother ought to be like a summer cabin or a winter chalet, somewhere to go when everyone needs a break. Including Grandma. The best thing you can do for Frankie and Grace is to take care of yourself."

This was the song Sylvia had been singing to Helen since they had met. Helen thought she had learned the refrain. Hadn't she found her dream house and fixed it up, set boundaries at work, allowed herself to play and fall in love? Surely, she had put herself first all the way along. But wait, now Sylvia was telling her there was more. Like *The Price is Right*, the stakes were always being raised higher. Now, she was being asked to cut her daughter and granddaughter loose, to let that little family establish its own boundaries and traditions. She was told not to be the Grandmother with a capital "G" who shaped every holiday, took hold of every weekday, and molded Frankie into her own image, selfishly hoping the child would find her indispensable and weep every time she left.

"That would be selfish," Sylvia agreed.

"I did it again?"

Sylvia nodded.

"Okay. I get the grandmother thing. It's hands-off."

"No. It is not hands-off," said Sylvia. "It is a question of being of service. How can you be of service to Grace and Jake and Frankie? How can you help them, encourage them to grow, without harming yourself?"

"Harming? That's a strong word."

"Yes, but you would be harming yourself if you made yourself accessible to the point of resentment, to the point of feeling used."

"Oh, but I never would! I love Frankie! Grace!"

"Oh, but you would, and quickly. You must know yourself well enough to see that, Helen."

"I'd like to think I wouldn't." The women sat in silence. It was late, very late. Helen looked over at Sylvia. The old woman looked worn. "I have kept you up too late. We should go to bed. I'll just use the loo."

Sylvia smiled. "You are even starting to sound like him."

Helen rose and walked down the hall to the bathroom. When she opened the door, she almost fell to the floor in shock. She remembered the small bathroom as being filled with mermaids, Sylvia's "girls." They had been everywhere— on the walls and soap dishes, toothbrushes and towels. But that had all changed. The bathroom had been expanded into a large room that gleamed with bright white tile. The sinks and cupboards were perpendicular to the door while the shower, nestled to the right of the tub, was encased in glass walls. The toilet was tucked away in its own little cubby to the left. The whole effect was expansive and brilliant. Helen felt as if she had entered the powder room of a divine opera house.

"I guess you have done a little remodeling," Helen said as she walked back into the living room. "It's gorgeous."

"I was tired of those old tubs I couldn't stretch out in. I consulted a doctor friend. He said to me, 'Sylvia, those dear old bones deserve a good soak. Go for it.' So, I did. It was a mess for several months, but we managed."

"Well, this will change your rental business, won't it?"

"I let go of that too. Tired of washing sheets. Cleaning bedrooms. Not that I minded having people in. I enjoyed it, meeting people like you and Grace. But I am not getting any younger, and I find that I tire quite easily these days."

Helen felt a twinge of guilt that she had kept Sylvia up this late. She thought she had been the only one going through dramatic changes. Why had Sylvia not mentioned any of this to her before?

"I didn't want to bother you, pet."

"Didn't want to bother me? But we are friends …."

"Exactly. And because we are friends, I need to share an observation with you. There never really was an opportunity to introduce my affairs into our conversations."

Helen's jaw dropped, and her heart exploded in her chest. She was both insulted and embarrassed by the remark. Hearing a similar remark from Frank, when she was married to him, had stung and brought out her defenses, but this comment from Sylvia, whom she so admired and emulated, cut her to the core. "I am the worst friend."

"Don't be dramatic. You have been preoccupied. What do you say we go to bed? It has been a long day. We can take a walk in the morning."

"Perfect," Helen said as she kissed Sylvia lightly on the cheek, thinking, *I have got to do better.*

Chapter 5

January 4, 2020

By the time the women woke in the morning, showered, dressed, and ate breakfast, it was already eleven o'clock before they set out for the park. The sun was shining a bright Carolina blue, and the temperatures were mild, as was often the way in the South in early January. Gladstone Park was not too far from Sylvia's house, just a half mile or so away, through the neighborhood of old brick ranch homes and mature magnolia trees. Helen sighed, remembering when she had left Connecticut just the day before, with tires crunching on the snow and windows iced with lacey, snowflake patterns from the frigid cold nights. Why did she live in New England? It was cold and gray most of the year. Expensive. Congested. She could easily move here into one of these one-story houses on an acre of land. Perdita could run outside almost all year. Sylvia would be nearby. But then, wouldn't she be almost as far from Grace and Frankie as if she were to move to Wales? And what about her job?

Helen inhaled deeply.

"You have simply got to turn your thinker off," Sylvia said as she held a green leaf up to Helen's nose. "Smell this."

Helen inhaled again, this time taking in an earthy, celery-like smell into her nostrils. "It's sweet, but dirty smelling. What is it?"

"Bergamot. It grows wild here. A renegade from someone's garden, no doubt." Sylvia took hold of Helen's arm, an act which Helen took as a sign of endearment.

"It's lovely here. So mild."

"We get the occasional snow."

As they entered the park, Helen spied two brown rabbits with white tails, standing on their hind legs. Their chocolate eyes were round and shiny as marbles. They stood as still as stone. Helen smiled as she imagined Perdita's delight in chasing such creatures, barking wildly as she chased them, zigzagging across the field by her home.

Her home.

Gone one day and she missed it already. "So perfect," she said aloud.

"Pests, actually. They destroy a garden."

Helen smiled, not bothering to explain her comment. "I think they are sweet," she said, "even if they are monsters."

As the women walked along the path, meandering, really, as Sylvia moved more slowly than Helen remembered from her last visit, Helen took the time to engage in her surroundings. Bushes with shiny green leaves bore cascades of bright red berries. Some trees still had their green, such as pines and magnolias, while others rose like candelabras, thick trunks supporting branches decorated on their tips by persistent yellow leaves, like flames. Everything was still and quiet, only the occasional brown leaves scratching the ground, pushed by the wind. Helen saw a bright red male cardinal dart through the woods and a small hammer-headed nuthatch, blue-black back glinting as it worked its way around a tree trunk in search of bugs. Helen breathed in deliberately, the sweet, damp, earthy smell filling her nostrils, and then exhaled purposefully again.

"Why can't life always be this uncomplicated? This simple and serene?" she asked Sylvia, who had taken a moment to stop and stretch her back.

"It can, pet, if you let it."

"I don't see how."

"That's because you are always looking for an outcome."

Helen paused as golden light filtered around her through the trees, making her look as though she were standing in a flute of champagne, then she spoke. "Sylvia, I appreciate your help, but that is really no help at all. I have a dilemma, a very real dilemma, and all you are offering me are Zen koans."

"Not Zen koans, pet. Those are really quite different."

"Well, improbable advice then," Helen said, stomping her foot unintentionally. "I need a game plan. I need an outcome. I need clarity."

"You know as well as I do, Helen, that no one can make that plan for you. That is between you and your Creator."

"What has my Creator got to do with this? I don't even know if I have a Creator!"

"Exactly."

"What is that supposed to mean?"

"Tell me, Helen, do you think you are running the whole show?"

Helen thought for a moment. "To a degree, yes. I have created my own destiny, worked hard for my life."

"Then tell me, what about Gerard?"

"What about Gerard?" Helen looked at Sylvia skeptically. "You are not going to tell me that my Creator brought Gerard into my life for a purpose?"

Sylvia nodded.

"Precisely. To teach you certain lessons about yourself. Right now, you are at a crossroads. Are you through with Gerard? Have you taken what you need from him?"

"That sounds so callous."

"Not really. Let me finish. Are you ready to let him go, or do you still have more to give, more to get in that relationship?"

The wind had picked up, and an unexpected chill permeated the air. Helen rubbed her hands together, blowing on them, regretting she hadn't brought her gloves. "More. I want more. I am not ready to give him up."

"Good."

"But what about Grace and Frankie?"

"Love doesn't disappear just because you are absent. You know that. Right now, you are feeling great love for them. It won't just go away."

"I know, but I want—"

Sylvia reached out and took Helen's arm.

"Listen," Sylvia whispered.

Helen listened. There was no sound in the air. Just the cold wind blowing through the trees, nuts falling to the pavement, squirrels in the branches.

"Ask this: What does God want you to do? That's the question you should be asking."

Just then, as if on cue, a spotted fawn emerged from the woods, stretching its slender legs over the bleached grass to stand on the pavement in front of them. It stood staring at the women, wide-eyed but unafraid. The underbrush rustled again, and out came another fawn and the mother. All stood like lawn ornaments on the path—deer and humans— gazing at one another. Helen held her breath. Finally, the doe and her offspring scampered off back into the woods.

Helen exhaled. "That was awesome," she whispered.

"That was a gift," Sylvia said. "From the Universe. A deer is a sign to treat yourself with gentleness and kindness."

"It is?"

"It prompts you to be yourself and continue along your path."

"You are making this up, aren't you? That deer and her babies didn't just magically appear in my life to tell me to be kind to myself, did they?"

"Maybe, maybe not. They did come out of hiding to take a look at you. They don't do that with everyone."

"You have seen them before?"

"Of course. We are old friends."

Helen just shook her head, not knowing what to believe but certain she liked the idea of being true to who she was becoming.

As they walked back toward Sylvia's home, Helen pondered. If she were to be true to herself, who was she? For so long, she had been defined by her job, her motherhood, and now Gerard. She felt herself honestly yearning to try new adventures, to dive into new love. So, what if she left the house to Grace and Jake so she could return when she wanted? What if she took her retirement early and moved to Wales? What scenario felt like a cashmere glove, perfectly soft and warm on her cold hands? No matter what course of action she chose, there would be some kind of pain involved. And maybe that was what God wanted her to learn, that there was no growth without pain. For Helen, the pain of leaving Gerard and all that went with that was greater than the pain of leaving Grace and Frankie. She could visit them anytime. To leave Gerard was to say goodbye forever, and she was not ready to make that choice.

"It's Wales," Helen blurted out abruptly as they rounded the corner to the house. As soon as she said it, Helen knew she had made the right choice. Giddiness rose in her like gas light bubbles, and she laughed. "I am going to Wales!"

Sylvia smiled, patting Helen's arm. "Well done, pet. Well done."

Chapter 6

January 5, 2020

Since all the "heavy lifting," as Sylvia had put it, was done, the next day would be devoted entirely to whatever Helen wanted. Sylvia suggested they might drive to Asheville, only two hours away, to see the Biltmore Mansion all decked out for Christmas. Helen leapt at the chance. Sylvia's only request was that Helen drive.

"I have to warn you, there will probably be snow," Sylvia added.

Helen looked at her, amused. "I'm from New England, remember? What's a little snow?"

"It's not you I am worried about. It's these damned fools down here who have no idea what to do in the white stuff."

Helen laughed. "I'll be on my guard." The women decided to make the trek at one o'clock, giving them time to eat a leisurely brunch in their pajamas, in front of the fire. Later, they would shower and dress.

Helen was torn. She wanted to be a gracious guest and chat with Sylvia over their stollen and eggs, but even more, she wanted to call Grace and find out how things were going at home. Had Perdita been eating and pooping well? Did they have enough firewood? If not, she should call Jack O'Toole. She wanted to remind Grace to eat the pepper in the fridge and finish off anything else that might go bad.

Mostly, Helen wanted to call Gerard. She had warned him she might be *incommunicado* while she was at Sylvia's. She didn't even know how many days it had been since she last spoke with him. It seemed like an eternity. She was afraid she would forget what he looked like if she didn't see him again soon. Already, his voice was like an echo in her mind, and she wondered for a second if he was real at all. *There you go, overly dramatic*, she told herself. *Of course, he is real.* She looked down at the delicate gold bracelet he had given her when he asked her to go steady. It seemed so absurdly real that she, at sixty-one years old, was going steady with a forty-two-year-old man who looked to her every bit like a movie star, and who had brains to boot.

"Helen?" Sylvia broke into her reveries. "More coffee?"

"I think I've reached my quota of caffeine," Helen replied, laughing. "Is there anything I can do for you?"

"Actually, there is something," Sylvia remarked casually, pouring herself another cup of Starbucks's Christmas Blend. "I have to go into the hospital tomorrow for a little thing. I had forgotten the appointment when we made the plan for you to visit. But it all works out quite well, as I cannot drive myself. I have to fast and I am afraid I might be lightheaded."

"Of course," Helen replied, her voice rich with concern. "Can I ask what it is? Nothing serious I hope." Sylvia brought her coffee over and sat down in the rocking chair by the hearth.

"It could be," she said. "Some years ago, I contracted breast cancer. It was never enough to take the damned things off, but I did have a lumpectomy. And another. And another. Then things got quiet, until recently. I have been dizzy and fatigued, not my normal self. When I went in for my normal check-up, they found something suspicious. Now they just want to take a closer look."

"Oh, Sylvia. I am so sorry!" Helen blurted out.

"Nothing for you to be sorry about. It is what it is."

"But, Sylvia—"

"No 'buts.' It is just where the wind blows you. None of us is exempt from the highs or the lows. The key is to ride the flow."

"Are you sure you want to go to the Biltmore this afternoon? We could stay here and rest."

"Absolutely not! I refuse to spend my last days huddled up with a heating pad in front of the fire. If you don't want to go to the Biltmore, I'll take myself!"

Helen looked down at her hands folded in her lap. She smoothed out the imaginary creases on her white silk robe. Here she was, all decked out like Carole Lombard in white silk pajamas with little silk slippers adorned by a feather puff at the toes, courtesy of Grace, stewing over whether to stay in her beach house in Connecticut with her grandbaby close by, or move to Wales to live next to a castle with a man who adored her and whom she loved in return. Meanwhile, Sylvia, dear Sylvia, was tough as nails, fighting this battle against cancer alone, only mentioning it as an afterthought because she needed a ride. If Helen had been diagnosed with cancer, she would have rented a billboard in Times Square and called on people worldwide to offer sympathy and prayers. Well, maybe not Times Square, but she would certainly let the people know who loved her.

"We are all different, pet," Sylvia said quietly. "We all have different ways of handling tough situations. Even in identifying a situation as tough. You are a talker. I am more private. To me, this is not a tough situation. It is just the next step."

Helen thought about this for a moment. "I would like to help you however I can."

"You are, pet. Just by being here, you are."

The trip to Asheville was uneventful. There wasn't much traffic, amazingly so, and the little they encountered sped along the clear roads, so the women made it to the Biltmore easily by 3 p.m. Helen drove carefully up the serpentine roads of the property leading to the mansion as the snow had begun to fall. Soon, she could barely see through her windshield, only enough to notice the heavy undergrowth and prolific rhododendrons were etched in white. Dark branches extended into the air like gloved arms. Shiny magnolia leaves were laced in snow. Everything was magical and still. When they finally arrived at the mansion, Helen gasped. There it stood, a monument in grays and browns. The color reminded her of *Jane Eyre*, and she imagined little girls in thin uniforms, drinking gruel by dim light.

Nothing could be further from the truth. Inside, glowing fires burned in every hearth, and magnificent pine trees laden with lights and balls reached high into the lofty ceilings of every room. There were plants everywhere—festive pink and white cyclamen, fiery Christmas cacti, and a sea of red poinsettias spread out around the conservatory, making their way to every tabletop. It was hard for Helen to get past all the Christmas finery to take in the more austere, and interesting, history of the house.

"This is fabulous," she said to Sylvia as she bent her neck to gaze on a tree that must have been thirty feet tall. It was covered in thick ribbons and old Victorian toys—miniature drums and bugles, dolls with Shirley Temple curls, metal trains. Helen was reminded of an old friend back home, Libby, who, at eighty years old, still dressed up as Shirley Temple for Halloween and sang with a group of singers, bringing music into old folks' homes. She, too, had had breast cancer, many times, and, like Sylvia, she was resilient, refusing to give in or give up a life she enjoyed so much. As one oncologist had said to Libby, "You are not going to let something the size of a golf ball ruin your day, are you?" She never did. She just kept living her life and doing the things that made her happy. Libby. Sylvia. Helen wanted to join their club, not with cancer, but just be an active participant in the *Happy as I Am Club* that allowed both women to view life with gratitude, trust, and hope, no matter what came down.

"You know the Biltmore hosted a Chihuly exhibit here not too long ago," Sylvia remarked as they gazed on a tree covered in exotic glass ornaments.

"Were you able to see it?" Helen asked, turning her eyes from the tree to look at her friend, who seemed no worse from the trip up. Helen wanted to ask Sylvia how she was feeling, but, somehow, she knew such a question would not be welcome, so she remained silent.

"I did. It was splendid. "

"I love Chihuly. All that glass and color. It is amazing what he can do."

"It is indeed. Well," said Sylvia, looking at her watch, "it is time for our tour. I should be able to get my ten thousand steps in today."

"Is that a smartwatch?"

"Yes. Amazing little thing. Tells me far more than I need to know, but I do like to keep up with my steps."

Helen was awed, but not surprised. Here was this eighty-year-old woman with who knew what kind of cancer keeping track of how far she walked every day. Not that age had anything to do with it—only it did. To maintain such commitment to health was definitely something to be admired. How often had Helen, using her age, aches, and busy schedule as a deterrent, opted out of going to the gym or even just taking a walk on the beach? (She actually preferred the beach.) For so many years, exercise had been a rock held over her head. She did it only because she should do it. She felt she had to do it to keep in shape. The presses and curls, squats and lunges. The miles running. Pilates. Planks. They all were a distant dream of late. More, in her memory, a nightmare because that part of her life was so driven by shoulds and musts. Today, she enjoyed walking on the beach at sunrise with Perdita or swimming in the Sound. She knew she would have to do better in order to keep up with Gerard who enjoyed day hikes and scaling mountains. He had even mentioned climbing at Machu Picchu one day.

For Sylvia, staying fit was a way of life, a part of her spirituality. Helen wanted to be there too. Not counting calories to maintain a perfect weight for vanity's sake but rather exercising and eating right in order to prolong health.

If regular exercise could help her live an extra twenty or thirty years, Helen vowed to start today. She could live well into her nineties, and she and Gerard would enjoy many things.

"Enjoying the tour?" Sylvia whispered in Helen's ear. The younger woman looked at her friend apologetically. "I thought as much. Turn your thinker off. Be here. Now." Sylvia patted Helen's arm.

For the rest of the tour, Helen did pay attention, picking up the standard facts about the colossal building: *Built from 1889–1895 on 10.86 square miles of land. The largest privately owned house in the United States at 178,926 square feet of floor space. Designed by Richard Morris Hunt and Frederick Law Olmstead.* Those were the bare facts of the estate, but they left Helen cold. What she wanted to hear about was the heart of the thing.

Sylvia was eighty, possibly dying of cancer. There was so much more to her than that. Years of memories with her late husband, their travels. Years teaching and helping young people, and old, find their way. So, too, was it with Helen. She was a sixty-one-year-old divorcee who taught Shakespearian Studies at Yale. For so many years, the trappings—the celebrity, the address, the degrees, her beauty—had been what defined her. Now, she was coming to know better. She knew that what defined her was her growing trust in the power of the Universe to guide her toward her true self. She had no time to waste, she had already wasted so much.

"Do you really think going to live with Gerard is the right thing to do?" she whispered to Sylvia as they stood at the threshold of the Vanderbilt nursery, all decked out with wooden rocking chairs and old teddy bears. "I will miss Frankie."

"Have you even asked the man if he would consider living here?"

"But I don't want to live here," Helen blurted out. "I want to start over."

Sylvia shook her head. "Helen, Helen, Helen," she said. "I don't think you want a geographic change. That won't solve anything. What you need is a spiritual realignment. A change of heart."

"But how do I get that?" Helen asked, on the verge of tears. "What do I do?"

"Just what you are doing, my darling girl. Ask the Universe to show you the way. And then, be willing to follow."

"Right now, you are the closest thing to a Universe that I have got. What do you think I should do?"

Sylvia just smiled. Then she took Helen's right hand and laid it on her chest, over her heart. The old woman closed her eyes and bowed her head. Helen felt the blood rush to her face. What would people think? And suddenly, she didn't care. Here was this old, dying woman demonstrating such love. Helen knew that was what she must do too. Demonstrate love. To Frankie. To Grace. To Gerard. To Sylvia. To herself. She wasn't exactly sure what that would look like, but she was sure if she led with her heart, not her head, she would find the right way.

"Thank you, Sylvia, for being such a good friend. For listening and understanding. For giving such good advice."

"My pleasure, pet. Now, would you like to take a walk around the grounds? On a snowy night, they are most beautiful."

✲

These woods are lovely, dark, and deep, Helen thought as she and Sylvia made their way across the courtyard. The snow still fell, though lightly now, illuminated by antique lamps that cast a pink glow. There were woods, but they skirted the perimeter of the estate. Helen didn't need to tromp around a literal forest to feel what she was feeling—peace. The world was hushed. She could hear only the sound of her own breathing, the crunch of their boots in the snow, the whispering wind blowing across the meadow. Pure magic.

"Look, pet," Sylvia said as they made their way into the garden maze where tall grasses stood in the snow, bleached feathery stalks rising higher than either woman. "I think these are porcelain berries."

Helen joined Sylvia at one of the evergreen bushes where she stood, and shined her phone light on Sylvia's hands. Sure enough, a bunch of bright purple berries hung from the branches like earrings. Iridescent, they glistened even brighter as Helen inspected them. "They are gorgeous," Helen concurred. "I love winter berries, the way they stand out against the snow. We had beautiful berries back in my garden at home." As soon as those words slipped from her lips, Helen felt a pall of sadness cover her.

"At your cottage? What happened?"

Helen smiled, disguising the uncomfortable way she felt. "No. At my old home. My old life." She didn't want to be back there in those years with Frank and her job, when Grace had been a baby, and life seemed so hard. Sometimes she wished she could forget the whole thing had happened. People always said life was like an onion; you peeled off the layers, and sometimes you cried. Her life seemed more like a banana. She peeled off the skin and proceeded to slip on it, ending up on her ass. Or maybe the banana had multiple skins, and she multiple falls. She had given up one life and started to build another, but she seemed to be in the same old predicament again.

How can I please everyone? she thought out loud again.

"You can't, pet. You have got to please yourself first," Sylvia said, taking Helen's hand in hers. "Haven't you learned anything?" Helen withdrew her hand abruptly.

"It is not as easy as you make it sound."

"Oh, I don't think it is easy at all, pet. And yet it is the easiest thing in the world."

"There you go again with contradictions!" Helen pulled on the rim of her hat, pulling it down snugly over her ears.

"The Universe is one big contradiction, Helen. Day and night. Sunshine and snow. The sooner you learn to live with the contradictions, the better. There are no real answers. Should you do this? Should you do that? As if there is some magic formula to follow that will lead to your desired result. That's just it, there is no desired result. There is only living in the moment, listening to your heart, taking care of yourself, and having compassion for others. And, at the end, you die."

Helen felt moved by the old woman's words but not convinced. After all, Sylvia had lived her life, and now she was on her way out. She had the perspective of someone who had traveled a long road and seen the destination ahead.

"On the contrary," she continued. "Life is not a destination but a journey. I will be learning until I take my last breath. And even then, who knows? Someone far wiser than I once remarked that life is not a problem to be solved but a mystery to be enjoyed. Enjoy the questions you have about your life right now. Enjoy the mystery. And meanwhile, enjoy the here and now. The berries. The snow."

Helen was, for once, speechless. She took a deep breath, inhaling the cold air into her lungs. She held it there for a moment and then exhaled. There was really nothing to say. She tapped the invisible watch on her wrist. "We have to be up bright and early in the morning."

Sylvia nodded.

"Best be on our way."

Chapter 7

January 6, 2020

Sylvia's MRI was scheduled for 7:30 a.m., but the old woman recommended they leave early for traffic. *A wise move*, thought Helen as they made their way down I-77. At 5:45 a.m. there were few cars, and they were all moving at a good clip. Helen knew, as Sylvia had told her, if they had left just fifteen minutes later, they would have run into congestion and jams. Cars would clog the road like faulty plumbing, and they would surely miss their 7:30 appointment.

Now, having arrived safely, easily, at the hospital by 6:45 a.m, they had loads of time to spare. Helen agreed it was better to sit in the warmth and relative comfort of the waiting room than be stuck in traffic in the cold rain.

While Sylvia checked herself in, Helen went to use the restroom. She looked at herself in the mirror as she was washing her hands. *Not bad for sixty-one.* But there was so much more than looks, wasn't there? Earlier that morning,

Sylvia had risen at 4 a.m., as she did every morning to do her morning prayers and meditation. The first morning Helen was in North Carolina, she had stumbled on Sylvia sitting rock-still on the sofa in the living room, a dozen candles lit, her eyes closed and headphones wrapped over her ears. She was listening to Pema Chodron, one of her favorites.

It is not like I don't believe in meditation and prayer, Helen thought. She certainly did. How could she not, with Grace and Jake striking yoga poses all over her house, burning thick smelling incense, and sharing with her the benefits of New Age psychology? Helen knew, intellectually, the only scoffers at prayer and meditation were the ones who had never given it a shot. So, what was her resistance? She would do a couple of downward-facing dogs and sun salutations, but, soon enough, she would stop doing the very things that made her feel so good. Helen admired her daughter, her friend, and their discipline. She admired their ability to stick with a thing and keep sticking with it. Prayer and meditation were not just a fad for them, an opportunity to show off in the latest athletic outfits. Prayer and meditation were a way of life.

The shrill beep of Sylvia's pager pulled Helen from her reveries. She opened her eyes and looked over at Sylvia whose eyes were still closed. They stayed closed until the nurse gently took the pager from her hand, saying, "Are you ready, ma'am? It's time to go back." The old woman opened her eyes, squeezed Helen's hand, and rose to follow the nurse. *How old Sylvia looks,* thought Helen, *in her blue jeans and flannel shirt, like an old farmer. Her face wizened like a rotting apple but soft as velvet.* There was a heaviness coming from Sylvia Helen had not felt before. *Is this it? Will this be the time the cancer has spread, inoperable? Is Sylvia going to die?* Helen felt a sudden rush of tears flowing down her cheeks.

A blonde woman wearing a badge and an artificial smile walked over to her. "Everything okay? Can I get you some coffee?"

Helen nodded her head as she blew her nose into a tissue the woman had offered.

"Cream? Sugar?" the woman droned on.

"No. No coffee. Thank you though."

"But I thought you said—" the woman pressed for an answer.

"I said everything is all right. Now please," Helen responded.

"No coffee?"

"No coffee."

"Well, I am here to help if you need me. Just let me know." Then the woman walked away to the next group of visitors who were waiting to hear the dreadful news about their loved one.

Helen felt overwhelmed. She didn't know why she had told that woman everything was all right. Everything was definitely not all right. Her friend was dying. Or was she? Helen didn't know, couldn't know. Was this one of those questions Sylvia had told her just to live with? It was Sylvia's job to be perky and optimistic. Or was it? Sylvia was too old and wise for that. She would never be taken in. Better to tell the truth. *But this is not about me,* Helen told herself. *This is about Sylvia. And Gerard. And Grace. Oh, Lord, why is life so complicated?* Before she knew it, Sylvia reappeared.

"All done. Let's go find somewhere for breakfast. I am starving."

"Did they tell you anything?"

"In a day or two, they will call."

"Are you … ?"

"Hungry. I am very hungry, pet, for blueberry pancakes, sausage, and orange juice. Now, does that sound like I am dying?"

Helen took Sylvia's hand. *Now who is comforting who?* "I hope you are around for a really long time," she said.

"That's the plan!"

Helen decided, over scrambled eggs and sausage, she would stay with Sylvia until the news came from the hospital. She wasn't sure how the old woman, so independent and set in her ways, would take it.

"That would be lovely," Sylvia responded, much to Helen's surprise. "I have some things you can help me with. But what about Yale?"

"We're off for Winter Term. I don't start teaching again for a few weeks. I'm sure they won't miss me if I'm gone for a few days. What about your guests?"

"Oh, there never were any guests. I was just setting boundaries … in case," Sylvia remarked matter-of-factly. Helen was mildly bruised by the remark but understood how the old woman needed to protect herself.

In case.

"I would have thought you'd have taken advantage of your break to be with Gerard," Sylvia said as she spooned a big helping of grits into her mouth. Helen smiled. She didn't want to tell Sylvia this was really no break, she had just arranged with the college to be away on "medical emergency." Though the emergency was not her own, this was where she knew she needed to be. She felt a responsibility to be with Sylvia, to see what was going to transpire, before she packed her bags and flew home.

The evening before, she had phoned Gerard and described the situation.

"Well, I selfishly hope she is in perfect health," Gerard remarked. "She has been such a Godsend for you."

"I am so worried about her," Helen said quietly. Not that Sylvia would be listening at her door, but Helen didn't want to share her concern with her old friend. Sylvia had enough on her plate already. "What if it's stage-4, and she has to go into Charlotte for chemotherapy? Personally, I don't think Sylvia would be likely to go that route. She would be more inclined to die like a Viking."

"Fall on her sword?"

"Wasn't that the Romans?"

"All right then, go up in flames on a raft in her swimming pool?"

"That's not funny. This is serious business we are talking about!"

Gerard sighed into the phone. "I know it is, Helen. Sylvia is a devoted friend. And you are too, by the way."

"What?"

"A devoted friend. I say you stay there as long as you need to. To hell with classes, papers, and overeager students sucking up to you."

"Now that you mention it, what about you? Wasn't the plan for us to meet during my March break?"

"Look, Helen, I am not going anywhere. You have a more immediate issue at hand. It is not as though I were a piece of prime real estate up for the next interested buyer. You have a mortgage on my heart."

"Wow. What a weird metaphor."

"You have encouraged me to become more colorful in my use of language."

"Don't blame that on me!" Helen laughed. "I appreciate it though."

"Ouch!" Gerard exclaimed.

"No ouch. I love you for your effort, Gerard. And for much more."

"I may have some news in the works. Get back to your friend, Helen. We shall talk soon."

"Shall we? And what shall we talk about?"

"You shall have to wait and see."

Helen wondered what that enigmatic remark meant: *I may have some news in the works.* She decided not even to go there but to wait and see.

Helen pushed her eggs around on her plate.

"No good? Try this," Sylvia said, pushing her hefty bowl of grits toward Helen, who took one spoonful. Then another.

"Are you through with these?" she asked, pulling the bowl in front of her. "These are delicious. I can't believe I have never had them before."

Sylvia laughed. "It's the butter and the cheese. But I am delighted to see you indulging yourself. I love that self-care." Helen polished the grits off like a hungry child. She couldn't remember eating that voraciously since she was a child and eating everything had meant revealing a cow or horse or sheep on the bottom of the bowl. When Helen was finished, she wiped her mouth with her napkin, laid it on the table beside her dish, and leaned back in her chair.

"You did that for me, you know," she said to Sylvia.

"Did what, pet?"

"You taught me to take care of myself, to love myself. Thank you."

Sylvia just smiled. Helen noticed the old woman had barely made a dent in her breakfast—one bite out of her blueberry pancakes, a single sausage link, and a spoonful of eggs were all that were missing from her plate. Helen reached out across the table. "So, how are you going to take care of yourself? You barely ate anything."

"I guess my eyes were bigger than my stomach. I'm sure that by lunchtime, I will have an appetite. I have some butternut soup in the freezer we can thaw. We'll have that with cheddar cheese and biscuits. Just thinking of it makes me hungry." Sylvia picked up her fork and started to cut an edge off a blueberry pancake. Helen reached out and laid her hand on Sylvia's.

"You don't have to do that," Helen said gently.

"Do what?" Sylvia asked, cutting away.

"Put on the brave face. This is me, Sylvia. Helen. You have always been straight with me. I am asking you to be straight with me now."

Sylvia put the utensils down. "Truth is, pet, I am a little worried."

Helen felt her stomach drop, but she kept her mouth closed, waiting for Sylvia to continue.

"I am worried about my yard."

"Your yard!" Helen cried, unable to contain herself.

"I am worried that I won't get all my pruning done and the garden put to bed before I am no longer able to do it."

Helen would have suggested Sylvia hire some high school boys or a real landscaper to come and trim everything up, but she knew better than to do that. To ask someone else to come in would be to sign a death warrant. She might as well be dead. Helen looked out the window of the restaurant. It was a bright, brilliantly sunny day against a China blue sky. So, it was January. It was still comfortable, though a little chilly. And the rain had stopped. What did her friend from Vermont say? "There is no bad weather, only bad clothes." Helen could dress warmly and certainly had years of experience pruning shrubs and tilling gardens. In her former marriage, her garden had been her refuge. The question in Helen's mind was, *Why has Sylvia put this chore off for so long?* Did this mean she had been suffering from the pains of her disease longer than she let on? If so, that could only mean one thing.

"Let's do it."

"Do what, pet?"

"The landscaping. This afternoon. You have all the tools, right? You can work up an appetite, and I will work off those grits."

"Weren't you due to call Gerard?"

"He can wait. He is wearing an 'Under Contract' sign on his chest. I am not worried."

Sylvia looked confused.

"Check!" Helen called, raising her hand and beckoning the server.

�֍

Helen surveyed the yard as Sylvia went to the shed to pull out the tools necessary for their project. Electric trimmers, loppers, gloves, a tarp, and an electric cord.

"Do you have a safety outlet?" Helen asked, eyeing the lawn still wet from the morning's showers. "A GFCI? Ground fault circuit interrupter?"

"I know what a GFCI is, my dear. And yes, right over here."

Helen was going to offer to help Sylvia as she plugged in the trimmers, but thought better of it and stopped herself. She could see the old woman was determined to take on this job by herself. *I've got to stop thinking of her as the old woman*, Helen told herself. *She is a person who deserves to be respected, not condescended to. She may be dying, but she has her dignity.*

"Be a help, pet, and keep the ladder steady," Sylvia said as she ascended the silver rungs, pulled the cord on the trimmers, and chopped off a number of stray branches on a rhododendron that stood as tall as the roof on Sylvia's little house. Helen's heart was in her throat. Here was Sylvia, eighty-years-old, possibly dying of cancer, standing on top of a six-foot ladder with a set of electric trimmers in her hand. Though, it was clear Sylvia knew what she was doing, had been doing for many years, Helen still worried she might lose her balance, break a hip, or—worse yet—her neck. How could Helen ever explain?

"Coming down!" Sylvia called out as she handed Helen the trimmers, descended the ladder, and moved on to the next bush. "The nice thing about living in North Carolina, you can do this almost any time of the year. The shrubs and trees are very forgiving."

Helen smiled. "I hadn't thought of that. In Connecticut, we are buried under a foot of snow. There is no way you would find anyone pruning past October."

Sylvia, who had taken the loppers to a couple of boxwoods, looked over at Helen. "You like it up there? Those long, cold winters? And you on the water. It must be colder than Pluto's balls!"

The comment made Helen laugh. "I love it," she replied. "It's what I know."

"I guess a person can get used to anything," Sylvia said, motioning to Helen to bring the ladder over to a rhododendron at the other side of the house.

"These must be beautiful in the spring. What color are they?"

"What, pet? I didn't hear!" Sylvia called out over the drone of the trimmers.

"I asked what color!" Helen yelled back, unnecessarily, as Sylvia turned the tool off.

"They are a lovely, soft pink dappled with a light brown, like a brindled cat. My treasures. We planted them forty years ago."

Silence fell between the two women like a veil. Helen wondered if Sylvia was missing her late husband, if she was looking forward to joining him soon. But Sylvia didn't seem the kind to indulge in such fantasies. She was far more practical than that.

"On to the fruit trees. Grab that ladder, will you, dearie?" Sylvia said, urging Helen on. And off they marched to the backyard where three gnarled and barren fruit trees clustered together like something from a Greek drama. "These girls deserve extra special care. In their lifetimes, they have produced the most delicious peaches, apples, and pears. I am afraid I have neglected them lately."

Then Sylvia did the unimaginable. As Helen stood holding the ladder, her mouth dropped open in disbelief. Sylvia climbed up into the first tree and made herself at home among the branches. Helen could not believe what she was seeing. How was Sylvia limber enough, strong enough to hoist herself into the tree? Helen didn't think *she* could have done that if her life depended on it. But that was just it. Maybe Sylvia's life did depend on it. Maybe this was her way of battling whatever disease was inside her, choosing to be active and vital. Sylvia was so full of surprises. That she was Superwoman was totally expected.

"Well don't just stand there gawking! Lay the ladder down and pass me the loppers!" Sylvia barked out like a teacher on the first day of school. Helen hustled to pass her the tool. "Now watch your head. Limbs are going to fly. It is your job to collect them and put them in the wheelbarrow."

As Helen ducked away from the flying branches and scurried like Quasimodo to pick up the debris, Sylvia started to sing.

"On the first day of Christmas, my tree love gave to me, a partridge in a pear tree …." Helen joined in on the two turtledoves, and by the time they had reached the twelve drummers drumming, Helen was breathless, wet from all the exertion. As they put away the tools and ladder, and dumped the wheelbarrow full of trimmings and branches on the side of the street, Helen thought, *She can't possibly be dying. She has more stamina than a bull.*

"If I am on my way out," Sylvia piped up, "at least the lawn will be done. Now, how about some lunch? I have worked up an appetite."

Helen, who was still full from breakfast, agreed to a cup of butternut squash soup. A very little cup, just to be polite.

"You don't have to do that." Sylvia winked, a grin on her face.

"Do what?"

"You don't have to be polite."

"How do you do that?" Helen asked, mystified. "How do you read my mind?"

Sylvia winked again. "It's one of my superpowers, pet."

Chapter 8

January 8, 2020

The next forty-eight hours passed uneventfully with trips to the grocery store, so that Sylvia could stock up on oranges and Chai tea; the hardware store so she could purchase screws necessary to fix a leaky bathroom faucet; the pharmacy so she could stock up on lotion and shampoo—none of that fancy stuff for her—and her medication which, hopefully, had been keeping her cancer at bay.

On January 8, Helen's phone rang. Not surprisingly, it was Gerard. Although Helen had spoken with him almost every day since her arrival in North Carolina, light conversations, this time, his voice sounded dark and full of concern.

"Any news?" he asked.

"None yet."

"This really isn't good, Helen. Maybe you could call the hospital."

"You know I can't. HIPAA laws."

"Of course. I forgot how uptight you Yanks are about sharing information." Helen detected a tinge of sarcasm in his remark.

"I honestly have shared everything I know with you. If you think I am purposefully deceiving you …"

"Not at all. But might you want to suggest that Sylvia contact her doctor?"

"I think she is in a little bit of denial. She wants to know, but she doesn't want to know," Helen explained. "Meanwhile, we have been running errands, trimming bushes …"

"What about your job? I imagine they are not too happy about this."

"I already told you, I simply gave my winter term class to someone else. I'll be back at Yale by the end of the month." Silence filled the phone. Helen heard Sylvia start to run a bath, humming to herself. "What is it you are really calling about?"

"I think you need to ask her."

"I can't. She is in the bath."

"Good Lord, woman. Do you want me to come over there to help you?" Gerard blurted out.

At first, Helen took his statement to be a criticism of how she was handling the situation, but then she thought, *Maybe he really wants to be here.* "You? Here? Why?"

"I thought that would be obvious," Gerard replied.

"I didn't mean it like that," Helen said sweetly. "It would be lovely to have you here, for the companionship, the support. The sex."

"There's my girl!" Helen could hear Gerard grinning over the phone.

"But what about *your* job? We can't have two unemployed people in this relationship."

"I have thought about that," Gerard stated seriously. "I am going to sell the house. I already have a prospective buyer. It is worth about two million American dollars. We will be set for a while if we live frugally."

Helen was dumbfounded. This was not something she had even considered as they moved along this relationship path together. What a huge sacrifice that would be, a sacrifice she was not sure she felt comfortable asking Gerard to make. *But,* she told herself, *I didn't ask. He volunteered.*

"Well?" he asked. "What do you think?"

"She may not have cancer. She may not need me."

"Better yet. I'll just come over and live with you."

Helen's stomach cinched. What had she gotten herself into? Here was this man who had only recently asked her to be his "best girl" now wanting to turn his life upside down to live with her. In her nice little cottage by the Sound. For a moment, Helen wondered if he wasn't just some kind of gigolo looking for an easy handout. But that didn't make sense. If he sold his house, he would have plenty of money.

"That's a long, pregnant pause," Gerard chimed in. "Have I said the wrong thing?"

"No, no, not at all," Helen replied. *Or maybe just lied,* she thought to herself. "But what about your job?"

"I'll find another."

Helen, seeing he was going to plow ahead with this course of action, decided to make a decisive move.

"What about us?" she said. "We barely know each other. We only just started going steady. Don't you think it's a little premature to change your whole life based on a friendship bracelet?"

"Whoa. Stop right there," Gerard stated. "We have known each other for going on two years. I have been in love with you since the day we met. All this nonsense about going steady—"

"You are the one who proposed the idea."

"I did. But," Gerard cleared his throat, "I never should have asked you to go steady."

"Oh," Helen felt the blood rush to her face and tears start to sting her eyes. *So now he is going to break up with me? But he just told me he wanted to live together. I am so confused.*

"I should have asked you to marry me right off the bat. But I was afraid that you would say 'no.' Afraid it was too soon. I am not afraid anymore. Helen Ferry, I am down on one knee, will you marry me?"

Helen's face broke into a smile. The rainbow had appeared after the storm. "Gerard Ferguson, are you seriously proposing to me over the phone?"

"I am. I know it is a terribly déclassé move on my part, but if you say 'yes,' I will sign the papers on my house tomorrow, fly over the next day, and propose to you properly by the weekend."

Everything in Helen screamed at her to just say "YES" to this wonderful man who was willing to give up so much for her. But she felt, too, an obligation to herself. It was important to her that if he truly wanted to marry her, he would propose to her with a blessing and a ring.

"You fly over here, get Sylvia's blessing, and propose properly, and we will see if I say 'yes.'"

"Done."

"And, Gerard, don't forget a ring. A nice one."

"Already taken care of. I love you."

Helen smiled. "Me too."

�֍

Sylvia emerged from the bath dressed in her old, lavender robe, her cheeks rosy, smelling like cherries. Rubbing her wet hair with a towel, she smiled at Helen who stood clutching her phone to her heart.

"Gerard?" Sylvia asked. "Isn't it the middle of the night over there?"

Helen nodded. "He is very dedicated. Besides, he had something important to tell me."

"From the look on your face, I assume it was good news."

Helen nodded again. "The best. I think. He asked me to marry him."

"And?" Sylvia queried. "I sense a second part to that statement."

"And he is flying over to propose to me in the flesh. With a ring."

"Very nice for you, pet," Sylvia cooed. "If that is what you truly desire."

"It is."

"Will you be flying back to Wales with him? What about your job? Your house? Grace?"

"That's the delicious part," Helen said, wrapping her arms around herself in a hug. "He is selling his house in Wales. He already has a prospective buyer! He is moving in with me."

For a moment, Sylvia's face clouded. She ran her gnarled fingers through her long, gray hair, separating the strands carefully and combing out any knots with the other. After a moment, she spoke.

"So, you won't be available should I need you."

"Oh, no! I didn't say that! If you need me, I will stay as long as you like."

"But, Gerard ... Helen you have made a commitment to him. You are asking him to give up everything, fly halfway around the world." Helen felt heat rise in her face.

"To be fair, I didn't ask him. He volunteered."

"Six of one ..." Sylvia replied.

"Well, why couldn't we both stay here a while and help you out? Anyway, it will be months before his house is sold. Quite apart from the fact that we have no idea what your situation is. Have you checked your messages? Did the doctor's office call?"

Sylvia placed her smooth, cool hand on Helen's cheek. "There is no good stewing about all this. Whatever is going to happen is going to happen."

"Don't go getting all Zen on me, Sylvia. Check your damned phone."

Sylvia laughed, shaking her head, then dug through her pocket book and unearthed her phone from where it was lodged between a water bottle, several pairs of glasses, a Burt's Bees lip balm, a travel-size hand lotion, and a pack of tissues.

"What else have you got in there? A lamp? An umbrella?"

"Very funny," Sylvia said as she pulled out her cell phone in its glittery gold cover.

"Why, Sylvia!"

"Why not? I like the way it sparkles," she said as she maneuvered her way to her voice mail. Sure enough, there was a message from the doctor's office, sent the previous afternoon. Sylvia looked over at Helen. "Are we ready?"

"We are," Helen replied.

As the message played, the stress in the room floated away like a loose balloon and popped. The tests had been clear. There were no new issues. Sylvia didn't need to return for another six months.

Helen wrapped her arms around her friend. "I'm so happy for you!"

Sylvia looked disappointed and confused. "I was sure there was something. I was sure it was my time."

"Well, it's not! So, be happy! You have been given the gift of more time."

"I am just sorry that I inconvenienced you."

"Don't be ridiculous."

"We have both learned a good lesson," Sylvia said as she made her way to the kitchen to put the electric kettle on.

"Always a lesson," Helen said, following her. "What is this one?"

Sylvia sat down on a chair in the breakfast nook. She looked tired and worn. "For some reason," she began with a sigh, "I let my imagination get the better of me. And my fear. I doubted that life would keep on blessing me, that I had used up my quota. I assumed that my time was up."

Helen listened to Sylvia with great intent. If even the wise Sylvia had spiritual relapses, how could she, Helen, even stand a chance? Life was giving her multiple opportunities for joy, so why was there always that nagging suspicion that somehow the carpet would be pulled from under her feet? Grace called it "Catastrophic Thinking." Evidently, Helen had acquired it in youth. But here was Sylvia, well-adjusted Sylvia, experiencing the same moments of doubt, a sickness in itself that could last weeks—months—and alter lives forever.

"The key is," Sylvia continued, "to be present in the moment. The lesson is to go where the wind blows."

"You have told me this before," Helen said quietly.

"And I will tell you again, for as long as I have breath. We do not control our lives. We make choices that shape them, but only God controls life."

Helen didn't know how she felt about such a declaration. Hadn't she shaped her own life—studied hard as a young woman, worked diligently to get a good job, to get the house she had now? Hadn't she been the one to rebound from Frank's infidelity and, later, death? And wasn't she now calling the shots with Gerard?

Sylvia shook her head back and forth. "Helen, Helen, Helen. You only *think* you have control. Life is actually going to take you just where it wants to take you. You can go willingly, or you can fight, making yourself miserable in the process. But in the end, it is the wind that wins."

Chapter 9

January 9, 2020

The next morning, Helen bid farewell to her old friend. "Promise me you will call if anything comes up," she whispered in Sylvia's ear as they hugged each other goodbye.

"You will be the first to know, pet."

As the taxi driver opened the door for Helen to get into the warm car, Helen called out to Sylvia. "You know, I came down here to get help with Gerard, but it ended up being so much more."

"Wind," Sylvia replied. "And Helen, tell your boyfriend that whatever he is up to, I approve." Helen nodded her head as the driver closed the door, and she watched Sylvia disappear through the wooden gate.

Helen's flight—originating in Charlotte, laying over in Chicago, and finally arriving at JFK International Airport—

arrived less than an hour after Gerard's non-stop from Heathrow. Miraculously, everything was on time. As Helen made her way down the cramped aisle, dodging packages and bags that tumbled down from the overhead bins, she wondered if Gerard would be there at the gate to meet her. She shook her head against the probability. He was probably in a different terminal, going through customs at this very moment. Surely, he would be detained longer than she, so there would be no handsome Welshman waiting for her on a bended knee, with roses in hand and a mariachi band playing in the background. *Helen, you are really the most ridiculous person I have ever known*, she said to herself. *You will be lucky if he finds you out by the taxi stand, freezing in the cold.*

"Excuse me, ma'am?" a voice called her. Helen turned. It was a young woman, just a college student by the looks of her, probably going back to school after vacation.

"I'm sorry. Am I blocking your way? Do you need to retrieve a bag? Let me try to squeeze—"

"No, no. That's fine. It's just … you're Helen Ferry, aren't you? The author?"

Helen was taken aback. No one had "recognized" her for a very long time. This moment brought back Christmas a year ago when Nicholas Kingsford had saved her at the airport carousel and asked for her autograph. Of course, look how that had turned out! He was her friend Micah's husband. They had all spent a lovely Christmas Eve with Grace, and ultimately the boys, as she fondly called them, had moved to Connecticut not far from her home. The world was so small.

"Yes, yes. I'm Helen Ferry. And you are?"

"Alison Maxwell," the young woman replied and reached out to shake Helen's hand.

"Well, what can I do for you, Alison? Do you have a book you would like me to sign?"

"Actually," the young woman continued, "I would like to ask you a favor."

Helen's curiosity was piqued. What "favor" could this young woman possibly want from her?

"I'm a producer of *60 Minutes* at CBS."

Helen tried to restrain her surprise but to no avail.

"I get that a lot. I'm older than I look. We are developing a series over the next few months on successful older women. I hope you don't mind being called 'older'?"

"Not at all. I am older, though not as old as some," Helen said, thinking of Sylvia, whom she thought to be the most successful older woman she had ever met.

Alison continued. "We are looking for educated, interesting women who can serve as role models for younger girls. I think you, with your background and experience, would be perfect! I saw a production of your play, *Couples in Conflict*, while I was an undergraduate at Yale. It was brilliant. I love the way it's been adapted to the current time. Being an alum, I have followed your career, and I really do think you have so much to offer. Would you be interested?"

Helen thought for a moment. Certainly, she was educated and intelligent, and she had achieved great success in her career, but what about her failed marriage? Her dead ex-husband? A foreign lover who was nineteen years younger than she? How did these fit into the picture she assumed she was supposed to paint as a "role model for younger girls"? The line started to move, at last, toward the exit door.

"Well, I am certainly very flattered," Helen said. "And I will definitely give it some thought. Do you have to know right away?"

"Soon," Alison replied. "Here's my card." The young woman tucked a small, white business card into Helen's coat pocket. "Call me, and we can discuss it in more depth."

"Thank you, Alison. You have given me something to think about," Helen said as they walked up the ramp and out into the terminal.

"Oh, there's my brother!" Alison said, smiling broadly. Then she turned to Helen. "It was a pleasure meeting you, Ms. Ferry. I hope to talk to you soon."

"Helen. It's Helen," she called out after Alison who was now embracing a tall, tawny version of his sister, both laughing and grinning as they walked away.

"Wind," Helen said to herself quietly, "where are you blowing me now?" That was when she saw him, Gerard, hustling through the post-Christmas crowds, black overnight bag slung over his shoulder. He looked a little goofy wearing his big overcoat and houndstooth, wool Sherlock Holmes cap, ear flaps down. She laughed at the sight of him.

"Sherlock," she said, kissing him on the cheek.

"Watson," he replied, dropping his bag and embracing her. Helen didn't mind that people might frown on this public display of affection; they were all strangers. Besides, she loved this man for all his eccentricities. She did hope, however, he wouldn't fall down on a bended knee and propose to her here in the airport. She needed to interrupt that possibility. Suddenly, she remembered Alison Maxwell and pulled the business card from her pocket.

"You will never guess what just happened!"

"What?" Gerard asked, kissing her lightly on her lips. "You have had an epiphany."

"More like an offer," she said, handing him the card.

"My darling, you're not …" he gasped as he read the card.

"Not what?"

"Not accepting offers from strange women in airports. Am I not enough for you?"

"Don't be so stupid," she said, pushing him away. "And don't make fun. She's a legitimate producer at CBS. She wants to use me on *60 Minutes*."

"Well, that is splendid!" Gerard exclaimed.

"Is it? What about digging up all that dirt out of my closet?"

"Watch those mixed metaphors, darling. They are not attractive. Anyway, of course it's wonderful! Sales of your books will skyrocket. You'll make even more money than you are now, which means I shall be able to live in the manner to which I would like to become accustomed."

Helen laughed half-heartedly. She wondered if that were partly true. Did Gerard only want her for her money, for the comfort she could offer him?

"Don't be an ass," Gerard said, as if reading her thoughts. Or had she voiced them out loud? She could never be sure.

Gerard picked up his carry-on and grabbed Helen's arm as well. They started to make their way through the crowded terminal.

"I guess this will all be over tomorrow," Helen sighed.

"Yes, back to normal chaos," Gerard agreed. "Thank the Lord I won't be doing this again any time soon! Now, tell me about *60 Minutes*."

"Oh, it is nothing, really. From what I gather, they just want to interview a bunch of old women whom they consider good role models for young girls."

"What a compliment! Of course, you are a good role model. Look at all you have done in your life."

"It's a good thing you didn't say I was old."

"But you *are* old, my darling, and that is what is so valuable. You have decades of experience and accrued wisdom that younger women lack. You have ridden out the storms of life and the halcyon days too. And now you find yourself in the enviable position of having a lusty partner, nineteen years your younger, who wants nothing more than to make you feel as young as you like."

"About that …" Helen said enigmatically.

"About what?"

"Nothing." Helen couldn't help wanting to take control. She didn't want him to propose here at the airport. But soon. She didn't want the magic to go away. "Let's get an Uber, shall we? It will be an expensive ride home, but I am not in the mood for changing trains." It was four o'clock, nearing the end of the day. Already, the light was slung low, and the sky was turning a peachy pink.

"Actually, I have made other plans for us," Gerard confessed.

"Really? And what would that be?" Helen was intrigued.

"Is there no surprising you? Just ride along with me, and you will see."

Wind, Helen thought to herself.

Gerard's surprise comprised tea at the Plaza, followed by a horse and carriage ride around Central Park, dinner at an amazing Thai restaurant Helen had never heard of, and a Broadway show. Well, not Broadway actually, but rather the last night of the Rockettes Christmas show. Helen's Christmas dreams were fulfilled. She had wanted to spend the holidays like this for so many years, but something had always gotten in the way, and she put it off, justifying her procrastination with excuses of too many people crowding the streets and the exorbitant cost. As she watched the Rockettes performing, kicking up their slender, muscular legs in unison, the sound of their heels clicking like castanets, Helen made a vow not to postpone joy any longer. If Gerard wanted to spoil her as his girlfriend forever, so be it. Life was too short to fight, to insist things fall in place in a certain way. Look at Sylvia and her scare. That could happen anytime. There were no guarantees.

Helen reached out for Gerard's hand in the dark. "Thank you so much," she whispered. "I couldn't be happier."

Gerard squeezed her hand back without comment.

As they left Radio City Music Hall, Gerard placed one arm around her shoulders. "You liked?" he asked.

"I loved," she responded, leaning up to kiss him. "Hotel?"

"One more stop," he smiled, taking her by the hand.

It was late when they reached Rockefeller Center, but skaters still spun and twirled on the ice, under the twinkling lights of the magnificent Christmas tree. Helen sat down by the side of the rink.

"Back in a jiffy," Gerard said, loping off. Helen wondered what he was up to, though she was pretty sure it had something to do with skates. Gerard was a hockey player who felt quite comfortable on the ice. Not so Helen, who found it difficult to relax with just a thin slice of metal under the arch of her foot. Still, if Gerard wanted to skate, Helen would skate. Perhaps he would sweep her up the way Cary Grant had taken Loretta Young in his arms in *The Bishop's Wife*. It had been a long time since Helen had thought of that, one of her favorite holiday films. Was Gerard just an angel who would disappear when his work was done? Whatever. He had given her this magical day and night. She would not ruin it with morbid reflection.

Gerard reappeared with skates in hand. "They are only open for another twenty minutes, but I figure we have time for a spin or two."

"I hope they gave you a discount," Helen said.

"Lace your skates. We have no time to waste."

In minutes, they were out on the ice, Gerard skating backward as he led Helen around the perimeter of the rink and then to the center of the ice. Suddenly, it was very quiet. Helen looked around and noticed the rink was empty except for the two of them. Only a dozen spectators stood at the edge of the ice.

"Gerard, I think it is time—" Helen began.

"Yes, it is." Gerard dropped to his knee on the ice in front of Helen. He took a small box from his pocket. Helen felt her face flush. She couldn't believe he was going to propose to her here, on the rink at Rockefeller Center, under the Christmas tree. It couldn't have been more perfect.

"Helen Olivier Ferry, will you be my wife?" he asked tremulously, as if she might actually decline.

Helen looked down at Gerard with tears in her eyes. "Yes. Why, yes, I'd love to."

He took her hand and placed a beautiful Monique Lhuillier diamond ring on her finger.

"Oh, Gerard, you shouldn't have."

"Hush," he said, taking her in his arms and kissing her. At which point, the crowd that had gathered around the rink burst into whistles and applause, stomping their feet in support of the couple. Then the skaters swarmed out onto the ice for one last song of the evening, this one especially for Helen and Gerard. Under the dark night sky and the crescent moon, Louis Armstrong's rich, warm voice crooned from the speakers, "What a Wonderful World."

This was more than Helen could have hoped for. She felt tears of the most exquisite joy stream down her face. "Thank you, Gerard. You have made me positively young again. I can't imagine anything better."

"Oh, but my dear, the night is young!" he said, swirling the ends of an invisible mustache. Helen giggled. It was past her bedtime, but she would try to keep up.

Gerard was true to his word. They returned to the Plaza, where he had booked a room for the night. They might have been newlyweds, all the attention they were getting. There were rose petals on the bedsheets, there was champagne chilling on ice, and two, plush white robes and heated slippers beside the bed. Helen wondered how Gerard had managed to pay for all this—the sale of his house could not have gone through that quickly—but she was too much of a lady to bring up the topic. Instead, she just sank into the luxury of it all, enjoying every decadent moment. If all this indulgence was meant to be an aphrodisiac, it certainly was working on her. By the time Gerard lifted her black cashmere dress over her head and gently removed her black leather boots and stockings and her silky undergarments, Helen felt more aroused than she had ever felt in her thirty years of marriage to Frank.

As she stood looking at him undress, she could barely restrain herself from smothering him with kisses from his muscular shoulders down his thick arms and taut stomach to his manhood, which now stood thick and ready for attention. "God, you are sexy," she said breathlessly.

"For you, my love. It is all for you," he smiled, eyes shut, as she slid down onto her knees in front of him.

Chapter 10

January 10, 2020

Helen woke sneezing. Not delicate, sweet sneezes that sounded like a silly mistake; these were big, raucous blasts that shook the bed and sent snot flying. As soon as the first sneeze left her, Helen became acutely aware of the headache that held her entire head in a vise, and, further, the aches and pains that gripped her body and wouldn't let go.

"And the chills, don't forget the chills," Helen said as she pulled the blankets up to her chin while Gerard ran her a bath in the huge soaking tub. "What time is checkout?"

"I have already taken care of it," Gerard called from the bathroom. "We are staying an extra night. Two, if necessary."

Helen looked around the room with its tall ceilings and extravagant chandeliers, the luxurious furniture and opulent floral arrangement. *Imagine, tulips in winter! How was Gerard coming up with all this money? Was he selling drugs on the side?*

"A gentleman never discusses his finances with a lady," Gerard replied when Helen posed the question.

"He does if he wants to marry her." Helen wrapped a soft blanket around her and made her way to the bathroom. It was steamy and warm.

"Be careful. It's hot." Gerard took the blanket from her as she stepped into the bubbly tub.

Helen sighed as she sank down into the deep water. "Just what the doctor ordered."

Gerard sat on the rim of the tub. "How is your head?"

"A bit better. I bet it would be even better if you would answer my question."

"What question was that? I have forgotten." Helen flicked a handful of white bubbles his way. They landed on his crotch. "You don't want to go there," he smiled.

Oh, but I do, Helen thought but refrained from commenting. What she really wanted was to hear the money story.

"It's really very simple. My father was an inventor. He invented many things and made a lot of money doing it. When he died, I inherited his fortune. I am actually quite an eligible bachelor."

"Not. You are taken, or have you forgotten that too?"

"Not for a minute." Gerard leaned over the tub and kissed Helen, while simultaneously tweaking her right nipple gently.

"Ow!"

"Ow?"

"Well, maybe not 'ow.' More like 'that was a surprise.'" Helen hoped she would recover soon so she could find out what other surprises he had in store. Just at the moment, though, she really didn't feel like going there. The idea of sex was, with the way she felt now, more of a mental desire than a physical craving. *Best to change the topic.* "So, exactly what did your father invent?"

Once Helen had emerged from the tub and was settled back into bed, surrounded by pillows and plush blankets, and Gerard had made her a "medicinal" mimosa in an oversized goblet, he sat in the armchair across the room. Lacing his fingers under his chin, with the two index digits propped like a steeple against his lips, he began. "My father, Michael Ferguson, was known to his friends and associates as 'Fergie.' He was the son of a steelworker, like so many in Wales. He happened to be very good with electronics. When World War II broke out, he was sequestered in a top-secret facility with four other physicists. They were charged with the task of developing a radar that could be used to detect air craft. The men, led by 'Taffy' Bowen, a fellow steelworker, built the transmitter that bounced off of objects to determine their location. Bowen was given the lion's share of fame for their efforts. But my father's contribution was no less important. He was responsible for helping to outfit the radar so it could pick up submarines' sonar, a factor that helped to win both the Battle of Britain and the Battle of the Atlantic."

Helen was mesmerized. "That's amazing! Your dad was a war hero!"

"Of sorts. But he had caught the 'inventors' bug.' He went on to invent all sorts of other gadgets, most of them useless. The one that made him the big bucks was the sonar cane." Helen had never heard of the sonar cane. She couldn't imagine that such an obscure invention could be responsible for Gerard's wealth. "Not as obscure as you think," Gerard told her. "The sonar cane replaced the wood or synthetic cane so often associated with the blind. Imagine, if you will,

Andre Boccelli walking down Fifth Avenue, not with a seeing eye dog or a wooden cane but a kind of translucent light sabre that can be elongated and retracted at will. My father's sonar cane took the place of the old methods and the stigma of the blind man in dark glasses tapping his way through the city and asking for change. The sonar cane gave the visually impaired their dignity back, turned their disability into a kind of superpower. It was very popular after World War II and is still used today throughout Europe, Scandinavia, and the British Isles."

"Why haven't I ever heard of it?" Helen asked as she tucked her knees up to her chest, wrapping her arms around them.

"The sonar cane never caught on in America, though I believe George Lucas stole the idea from my father when he created the light sabers used in *Star Wars*. My father was instrumental, however, in creating something that did take off, not only in the States but worldwide."

"What was that?" Helen asked enthusiastically.

"His percentage was miniscule, but the profit was so huge, he made quite a bundle."

"What was it?"

"Not important. The royalties ended with his death. As sole heir, born late to him in life, I was the beneficiary of his estate, which was worth quite a sizeable fortune."

Helen pondered. *What does all this mean? Why didn't he tell me? Was he afraid I would be attracted to him for his money? Nothing could be further from the truth.* "I wish you hadn't told me."

"As I recall, you asked," he replied. "Besides, we shouldn't have secrets, being engaged and all."

"Maybe we should rethink this. Maybe we shouldn't be married at all," Helen whispered.

Gerard threw his head back and laughed. "So, you would marry me when you thought I was an impoverished academic, but now that you know I'm rolling in dough, you're having second thoughts? You know what I think, Helen? I think you're afraid I've just gained control of our relationship, and you don't know what to do."

For Helen, that had a ring of truth. All her life, she had been the one responsible for making ends meet. As a little girl with absent parents, she took on odd jobs—babysitting, dog walking, raking leaves—to amass funds just in case her parents never came home. Later, in high school and college, she had forged applications, manufactured marketable resumes, and written papers for a fee. Money meant security for her, and power. As long as she held the purse strings, she was in control. When she married Frank, she had been the one with the higher-paying job. For years, she supported him and Grace, while he attended mortuary school and built up his business. All those years, she tucked a portion of her earnings away in case The Day should come. The Day had come, not when Frank died—though he had died later—but when he walked out on their thirty-year marriage. She was prepared to take care of herself financially. There was, too, the inheritance from her uncle that was nothing to be sneered at. Those funds had enabled her to buy her cozy house on the Sound. Physically, she was taken care of. Emotionally, she had a long way to go. Her spiritual life, which Sylvia often referred to, was just a glimmer on the horizon.

But with her dear friend's help, and Gerard's, Helen finally felt she was on the road to recovery. Until something like this came up. Just when she thought she was free of control issues, Gerard revealed he was a multi-millionaire and, *whoosh*, back came all the insecurities.

"I honestly don't understand you, Helen," Gerard said as he looked across the room at her and poured coffee into two china cups. "Most women would be thrilled to realize they have access to that kind of money."

"It is *your* money," she said curtly.

"It is *our* money. From now on, what is mine is yours."

Helen struggled inside. On the one hand, she appreciated Gerard's largess, but on the other hand, she didn't want to feel beholden to him. She had worked so hard for her independence; she wasn't sure she wanted to tangle it now. If she took his money, wouldn't she be giving him her power? The upper hand she strived so hard to maintain in all areas of her life?

Almost as if he could read her mind, Gerard came over to her, bearing a non-alcoholic beverage. "I know it's a lot to take in. We don't have to do anything right now. Here, drink some coffee."

Helen took the cup from his hand and took a sip. *Better.* She had almost forgotten she was sick, what with all the news and excitement. She wanted to call Sylvia, but the old woman had problems of her own right now. Besides, she would probably just scoff at Helen for making a mountain out of a molehill or looking a gift horse in the mouth. Her wanting to bolt and run was such a cliché.

Helen thought, *Maybe I can try it out on Grace. No, Grace would never understand. Besides, I am not sure I want Grace to know everything about Gerard and me. So, who else is there?*

Suddenly, the thought came to her. Nicholas. Nicholas Kingsford. Her situation with Gerard was similar to his with Micah. Though an actor now, Nicholas had amassed quite a considerable fortune as a chiropractor before entering into his relationship with Micah. She felt she knew Nicholas well enough to trust him with her secrets, to be totally honest with him about her concerns. As soon as they returned to Connecticut, she would arrange to get together. She'd tell him everything and get this mess clear in her mind before she ruined her relationship with Gerard forever. She smiled.

"Feeling better?" Gerard asked.

"Yes. Not one hundred percent, but a lot better."

"Good," Gerard said as he untied his robe, flinging it open to reveal his naked self. "Then you are ready for this!"

Helen's spirits sank. If she was taking his money, would this become an expectation? She liked it so much better when sex was spontaneous and not part of a package deal.

Chapter 11

January 13, 2020

*T*hree days later, Helen found herself sitting in a coffee shop across the table from the ever-handsome and engaging Nicholas Kingsford. Helen had first met Nicholas, a chiropractor at the time, in the Charlotte airport, at the baggage terminal to be exact. She had been reaching for her bag when something "twanged" in her back. She was momentarily crippled. Miraculously, this stranger whisked her away and healed her while confessing he had been stalking her to sign a copy of one of her books. That stranger, Nicholas Kingsford, turned out to be the lover, now husband, of one of Helen's old beaus. Micah and Nicolas had later relocated to Connecticut, near her home. Micah ran an antiques shop while Nicholas pursued a career in theatre. Their twenty-five-year age difference seemed to do them no harm. In fact, they were thriving.

"How do you do it?" Helen asked as she blew on her coffee.

"Do what?" Nicholas responded.

"You know. The age difference, for one."

"Oh, that's nothing. We don't even think about it, generally."

"Really?" Helen thought all the time about Gerard being younger than her. Would he leave her for a younger woman? Now that she knew he had money, would that change things? She was pretty certain Micah had reservations too. Nicholas was in his prime, as sexy as Jim Morrison. "What keeps you with Micah?"

"Love."

"Love?"

"Love. It is that simple. Don't you love Gerard?"

"Yes, of course," Helen stammered, feeling the blood rush to her face. "But it is *not* that simple. Something else has come up."

"Sex."

"Not sex. We are fine on that front," Helen said, disappearing behind her coffee mug.

"Glad to hear it. What then? Money? It is usually one of those two." Nicholas smiled a broad smile.

Helen was taken aback by his astuteness. Or maybe her face had just shown it? "Yes," she sighed. "Money. It turns out he is worth quite a bit more than I thought."

"Lucky you!" Nicholas said, lacing his fingers behind his head.

"Not really. It has complicated things." Helen went on to explain to the attentive young man all the thoughts she had entertained over the past two days regarding money, independence, power, lack of power, love.

When she was done, Nicholas leaned forward on the small table and looked her square in the eyes. "You sure do think a lot. So, what does Gerard say?"

"He says that what is his is ours."

"That is pretty clear."

"Why does that feel so demoralizing?" Helen asked plaintively.

Nicholas thought for a moment, rubbing his hand against his chin and then sipping his hot drink. Finally, he spoke. "Have you ever surrendered to love, Helen? Have you ever let someone love you, *really* love you? Or are you holding on to the reins because you are afraid that if you let go, you'll get burned?"

The questions took Helen's breath away. *Of course I have surrendered to love*, was her immediate response. But then, thinking, she realized she had never totally given herself to another. She had always held a piece of herself out in reserve, like her secret stash of money, in case she should be abandoned or abused, in case she needed to make a quick getaway. Gerard was the closest she had come. But total surrender? It seemed such a risky thing. "Very dangerous," was all she could muster.

"And so worth the risk. You will never know how connected you can feel until you let go and love."

Just at that moment, the jingle bells over the coffee shop door rang, and in walked Grace with Frankie all bundled up in a snowsuit with ears. "Mom?"

"Hello, sweetie." The women blew air kisses as they embraced.

"And Nicholas! It's so good to see you!"

"Back at you. Now, who is this little bear?"

"I know, right?" Grace laughed. "Frankie hates getting wrapped up in all this stuff. But it is freezing outside."

"She will survive," Helen said. "She needs to be bundled up."

"Speaking of being bundled up," Nicholas smoothly transitioned, "I need to get going. Audition at two. Keep your fingers crossed. This could be my big break." Nicholas reached down to give Helen a kiss on the cheek. "Remember what I said," he whispered in her ear. "Let go." He pulled on his coat. "Grace. Frankie. Nice seeing you." And with a jingle, he was gone.

Grace handed Frankie to Helen and started unwinding scarves and freeing little hands.

"Here, let me do that," Helen offered. "You go get something to drink."

"Thanks, Mom. Don't totally unpackage her. We can't stay long. We're meeting Jake at noon to look at another apartment. We got so spoiled staying at your place. Ours just seems so small and dreary. No place for this little nugget," Grace said, kissing her baby on the head. Helen refrained from comment and removed Frankie's little hat. Her wispy, chestnut hair, what little there was of it, shot out in all directions with static. Helen smoothed it down. "Can't have my little girl looking like a punk rocker," she said, kissing the baby's crown.

Helen had so many thoughts running through her mind. First, where was everyone going, so busy with appointments? Wasn't she usually the one with the tight schedule, racing from class to papers every day? Trying to find time to publish her own work in academic journals? Now that she was on leave, she was experiencing a new rhythm in her life. She had time to visit with friends, to stay and have coffee with her daughter, to hold her granddaughter on her lap. What had she been so busy doing all those years? Proving herself? Climbing the ladder? To what avail?

This is ridiculous, Helen told herself. *You are sentimentalizing things. All those years you spent working so hard were not wasted years. They brought you to this. To the point where you can sit at Starbucks with your granddaughter in your arms, watching the snow.*

Snow! Helen's eyes widened. Outside the coffee shop window, the snow was falling in giant, comical flakes, like something from a Disney movie. They seemed as big as Frankie's hands, and sure enough, when Helen took Frankie outside to stand in the magical shower, a flake landed on the baby's mittened hand, almost filling it. "Pretty!" Helen said, kissing the baby's pink cheek. "Snow!"

Frankie smiled, as the snow fell on her face.

At moments like these, Helen thought, *I am surrendered.*

"Mom!" Grace's voice called out gently. "Come in, now."

"You aren't mad, are you?" Helen said, handing the baby back to her mother. "I couldn't resist."

"Not mad, Mom. Frankie loves the snow." Grace sipped her peppermint cocoa. "So, what brings you to New Haven to meet with Nicholas Kingsford? Is everything okay with Micah?"

"Oh yes. It was nothing like that. More of a personal matter."

Grace eyed her mother with curiosity. "Personal? And you're not telling me?"

"It's nothing."

"It's not nothing, Mom. I'm offended you don't think you can tell me."

"Please, don't be. It's nothing."

"Is it Gerard?"

Of course, it was Gerard, she revealed to her daughter. Gerard and all his money. All that went with his being a closet millionaire. Helen might have felt happier if he had said they would keep their finances separate, but no. He wanted to share his life with her completely. She was not entirely certain she wanted to do the same.

"You could look at this as fun," Grace said. "You two could do a lot of good for the world, setting up a foundation or just supporting your favorite charities. Having money doesn't have to be about indulgence and excess, it can be about generosity and compassion. You could grow together as a couple." Grace finished her speech and turned her attention to Frankie who was starting to squirm in her seat. "I think someone needs a change. I'll be right back."

"From your lips to God's ears." Helen watched her daughter and grandchild head off toward the bathroom. Of course, Grace was right. Someone needed a change, and it was Helen. She knew she needed to make the leap from independent to—what? Not dependent. Not codependent. To being equally engaged in the relationship with Gerard. Grace had always somehow seen the bigger picture, ever since she was a little girl. But how? How was she to get over herself and her need to be in control?

Grace, who had returned with a much happier, fresher Frankie, took her mother's hand. "It's okay Mom. It's just old stuff that surfaces every once in a while. But you aren't that same woman. You are a new woman. You know how to let go of that shit. You are carving a new path. To me, you are an inspiration."

Helen was touched. She believed Grace's words. Hadn't she seen her life change in the last year-and-a-half, so different now from what it had been before? It wasn't just the house, the man, it was her way of being in the world. She had started to learn to trust the Universe. She had Sylvia to thank for that. And Grace. The only thing that had stayed the same was her job, and that was about to take a radical turn. She determined she would work one more year, and then she would retire, if she even made it that far. She had wanted to make it for her pension, but honestly, if she never had to, she would just as soon never go back.

"What's keeping you? If Gerard is as wealthy as you say he is, does your pension really matter? What is it, a few thousand dollars more a month?"

The idea she might simply walk away from her pension seemed as alien to Helen as walking away from Connecticut and leaving Grace and Frankie behind. There were some things that made her who she was, and sticking out her academic life at Yale was one of them. She was not a quitter. Nor was she a freeloader. The idea struck her as impossible, even as she considered it.

"So, there, you have your answer," Grace said as she tucked Frankie's hair into her hat. "Sorry, Mom. We have to go."

"Where?"

"We are meeting Jake on his lunch break."

"Sweet! Why don't you come for dinner on Friday? I'll make vegetarian chili."

"Yum," Grace said as she leaned down to give her mother a kiss. "I'll check."

"We will talk about *you* next time!"

"Mom …."

Helen watched them walk out of the coffee shop, the jingle bells ringing as the door opened and closed. She felt satisfied inside. She had shared some of her worry, and now she could move on and talk to Gerard.

❋

Helen was sitting in the den, surrounded from floor to ceiling with thousands of books. The wood stove in the corner crackled, shooting heat into the cozy room. The night was cold and still snowing since the afternoon. Helen was glad to have made it home safely, though really the roads were so well maintained that snow barely caused any inconvenience. Jack O'Toole, her trusted neighbor and handyman, kept her driveway plowed and her walks shoveled. All she needed to do on a snowy day like this was make some delicious soup and curl up with a good book.

And yet, Helen sat with her laptop in front of her, pouring over information, spurred on by her conversation with Grace earlier that morning. She hadn't spoken of it to Gerard yet. She wanted to be better prepared before she broached the subject with him. To Helen, the only way she could be reconciled to Gerard's wealth, to truly be a partner with him, was to invest together in something bigger than both of them.

"I have been thinking about the money. Your money," Helen said tentatively, breaking the silence in the cozy room. Gerard looked up from his book, the most recent Bernard Cornwall Helen had given him for Christmas. "Sorry to interrupt, but can we talk?"

"Fire away," he replied genially.

"You know how I feel …."

"I believe I do."

"This is hard for me to admit, but I am very protective of my independence. And I am very competitive. I find it hard to share, in fact, I don't play well with others. And I don't like being … let me rephrase that, I like being on top."

Helen paused for a moment, giving Gerard the opportunity to jump in should he so choose. Which he did.

"What is it you are trying to say, Helen? Are you bailing out of this relationship?"

Helen's breath escaped her. "Oh, no! God no! But I think I have come up with a resolution. Actually, Grace did."

"God bless Grace. Let's hear it."

"I think it would be best if we went into partnership and started a foundation or a non-profit or something and ran it together." The silence made Helen bite her lip. "Ouch!"

"Ouch?"

"It's nothing. Say something."

"All right then, what about your job? I thought you were determined to—"

"That's just it," Helen interrupted. "Though it is not in my nature, I am toying with the idea of retiring early. Honestly, I am so comfortable here with you, I would just as soon never go back. You could sell your home, move in here, and we could live happily ever after doing good things for the world. What's a few thousand extra dollars from a pension anyway?"

Gerard put his head back and roared. "Let me make sure I'm hearing you correctly. From not wanting any part of my fortune at all, you now want me to leave my job and home, support you in your retirement, and give my inheritance away to perfect strangers."

Helen felt the blood rush to her face. She regretted having brought up the subject. She should have listened to her own instincts and kept quiet, not blundered into this conversation. Now what had she done? "I'm sorry!" she stammered. "I was mistaken. I thought you might like the idea, but I see I was wrong. Let's forget it." She closed her eyes that were stinging with tears. She feared she had chased Gerard away forever. He probably thought her a greedy, conniving woman. Then, she felt his strong hands on her shoulders. She could smell his delicious cologne as he leaned down to whisper in her ear.

"Don't take yourself so seriously, my dear."

Helen whispered a little prayer of thanks to the Universe for putting this kind, understanding man into her life. That he was ruggedly handsome, sexy, and rich didn't hurt either.

For the rest of the evening, they sat side by side on the sofa, exploring the notion of starting a non-profit organization. Helen nestled up on Gerard's chest, their legs and feet intertwined. They talked about the things they cared about—the environment and climate change, potable water for everyone, food for the hungry, vaccines, medication, human trafficking, wellness programs, and education. Housing. There were so many areas of the world that needed attention, so many things that could be done, so many that were already being addressed, it seemed impossible to choose or to come up with any new ideas.

"It is overwhelming," Helen said as she ran her hands through her hair. I don't know where to start," she called over her shoulder as she walked back to the kitchen to retrieve them each another drink.

"I feel," Gerard began slowly as he took his beer from her hand, "that we need to find something that is personal to us, as a couple. Something we can really get behind with experience and enthusiasm."

"I agree. But what?" The fire in the wood stove had burnt down to embers. Perdita was snoozing on the couch beside them.

Helen yawned.

"Plenty of time for talking in the morning. Come on," he said, taking her half-full wine glass from her hands. "To bed."

Soon, Helen lay on the soft flannel sheets next to this man she loved, even though he was snoring. She smiled, inside and out. It felt so right to have him here beside her. They were partners, though not yet married. Soon enough. Soon enough they would discover a purpose for their partnership. But Helen knew in her heart she needed no purpose, not even a wedding really. She had found a companion for life.

Chapter 12

January 14, 2020

"*L*iteracy!" Helen sat straight up in bed and called out again, "Literacy!"

Gerard, who was still asleep, pulled a pillow over his head and mumbled, "Lunacy."

"I am not crazy!" Helen pulled the pillow off his head and playfully struck him with it. "I have had the most brilliant idea."

"Isn't it a bit early for that? It is still dark outside, and you haven't even had any coffee."

"Hear me out," Helen said, sitting cross-legged on the bed and pulling the pillow into her chest.

"Do I have a choice?" a groggy Gerard replied.

"What about we set up a foundation for literacy? We could start with children in the US and Wales."

"You're assuming there are illiterate children in Wales."

"You're not taking me seriously," Helen said as she left the bed and started brushing her hair in the mirror.

"Oh, but I am taking you seriously, which is precisely why I am putting the brakes on. In case you had forgotten, love, this is my inheritance we are talking about. I am still not convinced that we should be throwing it at some cause."

"Is saving the planet a cause? Is helping children read a cause? Is doing something for someone else a cause?"

"Well, actually, yes. They are all causes and noble ones at that. I just think we need to take our time and really investigate which cause is most needed, most suited to us. I'm not saying never do this. I'm simply saying let's slow down."

Helen felt chastised, as though she had done something wrong. She had assumed Gerard would be enthusiastic about entering into a partnership with her.

"We are partners, cause or not," he said.

"There I go again," Helen murmured.

"Yes, and it is one of the many things that I love about you," he replied. "Helen, you need to know that if giving all my money away would make you feel more comfortable in this relationship, I would do it in a heartbeat. But I don't think that is what you really want. I think what you really want is to feel comfortable standing by me just as we are. Money and all. It is not equality you want, it is serenity. And I am afraid that is something no outside machinations can provide."

Helen thought to herself, *There we go again. An inside job.* How often had she heard that from Sylvia and Grace? So now with Gerard, she was faced with the same lesson: work on the insides first, all else will follow. So, how was she to proceed? What was the next step on her journey to be? If it wasn't to be distracted by entering into some charitable venture, where was she to begin?

She decided to start by taking a shower.

Part 2

Chapter 13

January 15, 2021

With the holidays over, Frankie's first milestone passed (she was actually smiling now). And with Helen's leave almost over, she turned her attention to the next most important thing on her list. The wedding—their wedding. Helen knew full well that focusing on the wedding, in relation to working on inner peace, was like changing seats on the *Titanic*. It was a distraction, albeit an entirely pleasant one, but it was a way of keeping herself from being still and feeling the range of emotions that roiled inside her. She felt immersed in the surge of expectations, stress, and even fear over taking this giant leap of a new marriage. She didn't really want to feel those emotions right now, thank you very much, she just wanted to feel excited, expectant, happy.

Grace called it "false happiness." She said the only true happiness came when you had examined your life and let go of the baggage that held you down. Easy for Grace to say. She had only a quarter of a century of baggage to discard while Helen had six decades. Well, not quite, but a lot of ruts etched in her brain. She imagined getting in there to eradicate all the damage would be something like having a root canal on all her teeth. At one time. Surely, just coating things over with pleasant memories would make things all right? "But that's not the way it works, Mom," Grace had told her. "If you don't learn the lessons now and move on, the same shit will keep happening over and over again."

Gerard had arbitrarily chosen May 18 as their wedding date, the last day of classes for the year. The last day before her early retirement. At first, it seemed entirely fitting to Helen that her wedding and her last day of work should fall on the same day. She imagined herself giving one final lecture, bowing to a standing ovation from her students, and then quickly whisking herself away to change into her wedding clothes. But then, she realized it wouldn't really be her last day of work. There would be graduation, and then she would have loads of papers to grade and grades to register before she signed off permanently on June 1. She couldn't get married the weekend before because it was Mother's Day weekend, and she didn't want to steal the limelight from Grace. Maybe she could just wait until June, but June brides were such a cliché. July was too hot. August was the anniversary month of her marriage to Frank, and September seemed too far away.

Helen clutched her hair in despair and plopped her head down on the desk in front of her.

Through the baby monitor, she heard Frankie's sweet voice, cooing. Frankie was just over one month old now, chestnut curls and big blue eyes. She reminded Helen of Pearl, that little symbol of Hope in Nathaniel Hawthorne's classic novel, *The Scarlet Letter*. Of course, Grace was no adulteress, so the similarities ended there.

Helen had agreed to watch Frankie while Grace and Jake took the day for themselves. They were cashing in on the "Grandma coupons" Helen had given them for Christmas—a book of twenty-five babysitting coupons to be used between January 1 and June 1. It was a suggestion Sylvia had made. Setting boundaries would protect Helen from herself and her desire to please Grace, and curb Grace's tendency to take advantage of her mother's soft spot for the baby. Helen thought the idea a bit crass, but no noses were put out of joint by it. In fact, Grace and Jake were delighted.

"It takes the guilt away," Jake had commented. "You have given us permission to use you."

"You know I love watching Frankie," Helen replied as she sipped her chardonnay. The kids had returned from their outing, and Frankie was happy in her bouncy chair, watching the flames lick the wood in the fireplace on this blustery winter day.

"Of course you do, Mom. It's just this way is better. With boundaries. We won't overuse you, and you won't resent us."

"Oh, I would never resent you," Helen said quickly, though she knew that was not true. There had been a time during this first month when she had been called on so much that she felt like a new mother herself (which was why she had leapt at the idea when Sylvia suggested it).

Sylvia. Helen realized then she hadn't heard from Sylvia in a few weeks, which was nothing unusual, but with her recent scare, Helen was concerned. Just as she picked up her cell phone to dial, she heard Frankie's plaintive cry. That could only mean one of three things: soiled diaper, hunger, or boredom. Much like her own alarms. Helen walked back into the living room, and there was Gerard lifting Frankie up in his arms.

"Well, there's the culprit," he said, holding the baby high and sniffing her bottom. Helen found the gesture both disgusting and endearing at the same time.

"You want me to change her?" she asked, following him into the nursery.

"I've got this. You take care of whatever you were doing." He laid the baby down on the changing table and released the diaper. "Wow! I am going to need a firehose for this. What did you eat, you little angel? Liver and onions?"

Helen smiled. *Men are such babies when it comes to babies*, she thought. But she was grateful Gerard was willing to pitch in without having to be asked. Just as he pitched in with the cooking and the cleaning. He was so thoughtful and generous. So handsome and sexy. So rich. Once again, Helen was plagued with doubt. Why was he here with her?

She looked over at him holding the little girl against a burping rag on his shoulder, patting her back gently. "Now that you are emptied out, shall we fill up that tummy again, eh, Frankie? What do you say? Another bottle?" The baby just cooed, lifting her head slightly to look at him.

"She knows you," Helen said. "She knows your voice. She likes you."

"To know me is to like me," Gerard smiled.

"It certainly is. Gerard are you sure …." Helen began.

"Another bottle? Absolutely."

"Be serious a minute. Are you sure you want to marry me? You are so young and handsome. You could have any woman."

"You are right. I could. I could have any woman that I desired." Gerard put Frankie in her baby seat, then walked over and took Helen in his arms. "But I don't want any woman. I want you. Call me crazy, but I find the package of you—your brains, your beauty, your blasted insecurities—absolutely irresistible. You are the woman of my dreams. I want you to be my wife." Then he kissed her, gently at first and then passionately. All Helen's fears were assuaged—if only temporarily. Frankie kicked her little legs and laughed.

"Are you laughing at us?" Gerard turned toward the baby. "No milk for you," he announced, obviously a little too sternly because the baby's face dissolved into a pout, complete with curled lip. "JK, JK." Gerard poked her tummy. "Bottle coming right up!" Sunlight spread across Frankie's face. "That's my girl!"

Helen watched the interaction, amazed. Frank had never been this good with Grace. Come to think of it, he hadn't even really liked Grace as a baby. He said he had no time for kids until they were old enough to ride a bike and tie knots. No wonder they never had another. One was more than Frank could take. Helen began to feel resentment brewing but caught herself. No point in speaking ill of the dead. Besides, the decision not to have a second child had been as much hers as Frank's. She saw a second baby as an obstruction to all she hoped to achieve. Her thinking then was so far from where it was today. Today, she saw Frankie not as an interruption, keeping her from doing the things she wanted to do. Instead, Frankie *was* the thing she wanted to do; she was the gift that took Helen out of herself.

Helen was reminded of Sylvia who seemed to see everything as a gift. They hadn't spoken for a long time, and Helen wondered if her old friend was all right. Had she fallen down while dismantling the Christmas tree? Helen picked up her phone to dial, but just then, Gerard, who was now busy feeding Frankie, spoke.

"So, did you make any headway on a date?"

"For the wedding?"

"Of course."

"Not really. I had wanted April 23, Shakespeare's birthday, but that is a Thursday. And May is just too busy with finals and graduation. I really don't have time to plan anything before then. And June is a cliché. July is too hot. August doesn't work for me. I really don't see an opportunity until Columbus Day weekend, and even then, there will be no honeymoon right away."

"What happened to the early retirement?" Gerard asked, eyebrows furled. "I thought you would be free by June for our honeymoon."

"I am just saying. Even if I retire, June is a cliché, and July is too hot and sticky."

"There will be a honeymoon," Gerard asserted.

"Well, not right away. It all just seems so impossible. I don't see how people do it."

"Perhaps not impossible," Gerard said, wiping milk that had dribbled down Frankie's chin. "Let's put the wedding and honeymoon together. Let's elope to Las Vegas. We could get hitched and then hike the canyons around the city. Gamble a little. See some shows."

"Sounds fun. When?"

"How about we fly out tomorrow, and we get the honeymooning in before you have to be back at Yale at the end of the month?"

Helen thought for a moment. It all sounded so exciting. They could stay at the Venetian, something she had always wanted to do. Take a romantic ride in a gondola. Surely, there were some hikes that weren't snow-laden. But then, looking over at Frankie, Helen realized she would miss the baby, and Grace. She had wanted to have a party after the wedding and invite all her friends. Micah and Nicholas. Jack O'Toole. Her colleagues at school. The Habitat crew. If she married Gerard in Vegas, no one would be there to celebrate with her. Just red-eyed gamblers, nursing their losses in a glass of gin.

"Nothing saying we can't have a party when we return."

Helen thought some more. Vegas? The trip? The expense was no issue, but the time? If she was going to get married in winter, why not elope to a real Winter Wonderland? Go skiing and skating. Drink mulled wine by the fire. Make love under soft down comforters and wake to the smell of cinnamon rolls.

"You've got that look," Gerard smiled. "I have a feeling you're thinking something extravagant. The Caribbean? Zurich? Montreal?"

"Closer. I'm thinking Vermont. It's close. It's beautiful. It's quiet and simple."

"Vermont," Gerard pondered. "I have never been to Vermont. Of course, I have seen *White Christmas*."

"Vermont is beautiful this time of year."

"Then Vermont it is! When are the kids coming back to collect this little one?" Frankie's little face buckled up, and she began to cry. "Just teasing, lambie! We love you! Now who is a darling child?" While Gerard consoled the unhappy child, pacing the floor and bouncing her up and down, Helen called the town offices in one of the southern-most towns in the state to inquire about obtaining a marriage license. The process turned out to be much simpler than she had anticipated, and she was suddenly overwhelmed with the reality that in three days, when she went to sleep, she would be sleeping with her husband beside her.

Chapter 14

January 17, 2020

Two days later, Helen and Gerard, with Perdita in tow, piled into Helen's Range Rover and headed north to a little town in Vermont called Brookdale. As they passed the snow-capped pines that shook sparkling dazzle from their branches along the Parkway, Helen was reminded of something Sylvia had once said: *There's magic in everything, and it's magic we are a part of.* Certainly, Helen felt the magic at work in her life. Who would have thought, two years ago, she would be eloping into this wonderland with the love of her life, soon to be her husband? Who could have imagined Helen would have adopted a scruffy dog only to have her turn out to be her best friend? Frankie? Who could have imagined Grace, grown up and mature? Sometimes, life just dishes out miracles. But like Sylvia had said, there are miracles all around us and recognizing that we are the greatest miracles of all were what moved us down the river to where the waters were calm and clear, where we could relax and enjoy our brief stint on this planet.

"Thank you, Sylvia," Helen whispered.

"What was that, love?" Gerard asked.

"Nothing. I just need to call Sylvia," Helen said as she dialed. She was met with a hollow ring that rang and rang until it went to voicemail. Sylvia's gravelly voice and curt message made Helen smile. *You know the drill. And if you don't, you shouldn't be playing with that phone.*

"It's me, Syl. Helen. Just checking in. Give me a call when you have the chance."

"Now, where are we headed to?" Gerard asked.

Helen had discovered, in looking for someplace for them to stay, there were surprisingly few motels in the area. Even fewer hotels. All of them were booked, she imagined, with skiers coming up north to enjoy the fresh snow that had fallen overnight. So, she had gone online and found what she hoped would be the perfect rental home. She was hoping for something with enough privacy so she and Gerard wouldn't be met with judgement as they emerged from their wedding night's festivities. The house she found was a small cape, close enough to the road so they wouldn't get snowed in, but remote enough so they could enjoy the beautiful views. Or so the owners had written in their text. The beauty of it was, they had converted the upper floor of their barn into an apartment. Pictures showed a clean, bright space with kitchenette, bath, and picture windows looking out over the mountains. A bright red iron wood stove in the corner filled the space with warmth and cheer. The couch pulled out into a king-sized bed, more than enough room for the two of them. It was perfect. Better yet, it was available.

Gerard pulled into the snowy driveway, wheels crunching on the snow, at four o'clock in the afternoon. Check-in time. Already the night was falling, and the snow was turning blue. The cold air fastened their nostrils together as Helen jogged in place, wishing she had worn a heavier, less stylish, pair of pants.

"Well, here we are!" Gerard said as he chirped the car off, though from the looks of it, there was no one around for miles. "Looks charming, don't you think?"

Indeed, charming it was with white mini lights strung in the trees and bushes and on the front porch. A big wreath with a plaid bow rested on the door. Helen thought, *Someone hasn't heard Christmas is over*, and then scolded herself mentally for having such critical thoughts.

The truth was, Helen could not stop thinking. *Tomorrow, I will be married. Maybe not in a church, but we will have a license, and I will be Helen Ferry Ferguson. Only I won't, I won't take his name.* She never had with Frank. Why would she with Gerard? Then again, why would she not?

"Well, are we going in?" Gerard asked, his breath frosty in the air. "It's bloody cold out here."

Helen knocked on the door.

Helen told herself she hadn't known what she expected. Actually, she did. She expected Sylvia, whom she and Grace had spent Christmas with in her rental home a year ago, to answer the door. *Sylvia! I must call Sylvia again*, she told herself as they stood outside waiting for someone to come to the door.

Suddenly, the door swung open and two people—an elderly woman with a velvet soft face that resembled a tawny owl, and a tall, thin man as straight as a rake, wearing heavy boots and a barn coat—welcomed them as two miniature border collies ran circles around the guests. Perdita was yelping wildly in the car.

"Well, come in, come in," the old woman motioned to Helen and Gerard. "Tom will put your bags in the honeymoon suite," she said, winking, "while I fix us some nice hibiscus tea."

Helen almost burst out laughing. Were all rental hosts this unique? She looked around the house, which was as cozy a place as she had ever seen. Dozens of hot pink cyclamens, their fat leaves and delicate blooms leaning toward the southern light, covered end tables, coffee tables, and even the dining room table. "He gives me one every Christmas. Has for years. It's become quite a fetish, I'd say. But I love them. "

"They are beautiful," was Helen's meek reply.

A roaring fire spat and crackled in the hearth, sending out chutes of heat that encouraged Helen to take off her hat and gloves. As she inhaled, she recognized the house smelled sweet, not sugary sweet but baking sweet, a smell Helen couldn't quite name.

"What's that delicious—" she began.

"It's bread, dearie. I am making my week's-worth of whole wheat loaves. Tom loves it warm with butter and strawberry jam."

So, do I! thought Helen. She turned to Gerard, but he was gone.

"He went to help Tom with the bags. He will be right back. Shall we rescue that little dog of yours before she turns into a pupsicle? She can meet Portia and MacDuff."

Helen laughed. This was too much of a coincidence for her to bear. The old woman looked at her curiously, almost offended. "No, no, no! I am not laughing at the dog's names. Well, I am actually. I named my little girl Perdita. She was lost …"

"… and you found her. *Twelfth Night*, act 1, scene 4. I understand."

Helen shoved her gloves and hat in her coat pockets. "I don't believe we have properly met. I am Helen Ferry."

The old woman smiled in recognition. "Of course you are, dearie. Shakespeare scholar, Yale. Something of a celebrity."

Helen bowed her head slightly. She hadn't banked on being identified. She had wanted just to be a newlywed without all the baggage of the rest of her life.

"And I am Catherine Forester. Call me Cat. Shakespearian scholar Emeritus at Bennington College."

"What a coincidence that of all the rental homes in Vermont, I should pick yours!" Helen exclaimed.

"Not a coincidence at all, my dear. It is all part of a larger plan."

The whistling tea kettle suddenly emitted a loud shriek. The dogs jumped off their cozy seats on the big couch in the living room, yapping their way into the kitchen. Cat bustled to the stove while Helen headed for the door to retrieve Perdita from the car. Just as she placed her hand on the knob to pull the door open, in came Tom and Gerard, who held the shivering Perdita in his arms. Tom was laden down with wood.

"Got to warm this little pupsicle up," Tom grinned. "She's a friendly little thing."

Perdita, in response, squirmed her way out of Gerard's arms and immediately bounded off to greet Portia and

MacDuff. After a little butt-sniffing and cautious circling, they all agreed to be friends.

Gerard kissed Helen on the top of her head. "The place is lovely. Nicer than the photos," he whispered in her ear. "I think you will love it."

"Everyone, come sit," Cat announced, carrying a tray of steaming tea and a plate piled high with slices of bread, still warm from the oven. Butter and homemade strawberry jam made up the snack. "Organic," Cat said. "Everything. It is the only way to go." She winked at Helen, who began to wonder if maybe the wink wasn't actually a tic. For several minutes, they sat, quietly sipping their tea—a red hibiscus blend which, though unsweetened, tasted like warm juice, something one might find on the Islands—and eating slices of warm whole wheat bread dripping with butter and strawberry jam.

"If you would prefer honey …." Cat offered, but everyone agreed strawberry jam was perfect for a cold winter's night, bringing back, as it did, memories of summer when the berries were plentiful and the sun warm and golden.

Gerard was in Heaven. "At last, a proper tea!" he exclaimed. "I haven't had a proper tea since I left Wales."

"Perhaps you would prefer black tea?" Cat asked.

"Nonsense. This is perfect as it is. My compliments to the chef," he said, raising his cup.

"When did you leave Wales?" Cat, who seemed to be the talker of the pair, asked.

"Let's see. A week ago."

They all laughed. Helen calculated in her head. Had it only been a week? Gerard had come on New Year's Eve, then left on the third when Helen had flown down to Sylvia's. She had stayed there for seven days, and Gerard had flown in on the tenth. Today was the seventeenth. So, yes, he was right.

I really must call Sylvia, Helen told herself. *Tonight. In fact, right now.*

"I am so sorry," she said as she rose from the table. "But I really must make a quick call. How is the reception here?"

"Spotty at best," Cat piped in.

"We don't use cell phones. There is a land line over in the hall. You'll get reception there," Tom advised.

As Sylvia walked from the room, she overheard Cat say to her husband, "She's a very busy woman. Helen Ferry. You know, the Shakespeare expert at Yale."

"You don't say," he replied, taking a sip of his tea. "Small world. And who are you?" he said, turning to Gerard. "Benedict Cumberbatch?" Gerard could barely keep from spitting out his tea.

The phone at Sylvia's house rang and rang. Just as she was about to hang up, an unfamiliar voice answered the phone. "Hello?"

"Hello! This is Helen Ferry. I am a friend of Sylvia's. Is Sylvia there? Is everything all right?"

"Are you a member of the family?"

"No, I am not a direct relation, but I am a close friend. And I am concerned about Sylvia. Will you please tell me what is going on?"

There was a long silence. Finally, after Helen had had time to expect the worse—murder, heart attack, car accident—the voice came back on. "Just a minute, ma'am."

In seconds, another unfamiliar voice came on.

"Mrs. Ferry?"

"Ms. Ferry, but soon to be Mrs. Ferguson." Helen had no idea why she was revealing details about her life to this stranger, but the truth was, she thought if she was intimate with him, he might cut through the tape and tell her what had happened.

"This is Captain Johnson, from the White Oaks Police. Are you Helen Ferry from Madison, Connecticut?"

"Yes, of course I am!" Helen felt her heart pounding in her chest. She knew the news would not be good.

"I'm sorry to report that Ms. Sylvia had an accident while up on a ladder in a tree. She appeared to be pruning branches when she slipped and fell on the pruning shears. We don't think she ever achieved consciousness. By the time her neighbor found her, she was long gone. I am so sorry for your loss."

Wait! Wait! Sylvia can't be gone! Helen wanted to scream. *If only I had called her, maybe she wouldn't have climbed that tree.*

"She left a letter here addressed to you. I will send it on," the captain stated. "It seems like she doesn't have much family. Husband dead. No kids. No living cousins that we can find. You are the only contact we have come across. Would you be able to come down and settle things up? I hate to see all this beautiful stuff just get trashed. And, of course, there is the funeral."

"What about her executor? Surely, she left a will. Sylvia was very practical."

"That's just it. According to her lawyer, Sylvia changed her will in the last month, much to his dismay. Didn't she tell you?"

"Never mentioned a word. Did she appoint me? I am afraid I am so busy." Helen could hear Sylvia's words ring in her head. *Too busy to look after an old friend? You always said that you would be there for me.* Helen couldn't think. Everything was rushing in on her. The wedding. Now, a funeral. How was she going to manage returning to school in nine days, clearing up Sylvia's estate in less than a week, and celebrating her marriage and a honeymoon? She ran her fingers through her hair in a desperate effort for clarity.

"We'll be in touch, as soon as we can verify her will," the captain said. "Of course, the sooner you could get down here, the better."

Helen imagined the closets full of memorabilia, the desk stuffed with papers. What was she supposed to do with all this stuff? Who would want it anyway? Grace. Grace might like some things. Maybe she and Frankie could come down to North Carolina with her. They could sort through stuff, learn more about Sylvia, scatter her ashes (and Henry's) at the beach. It might not be so bad—just delayed nuptials and another leave from school. Hell, she should probably just resign and have done with it. But Grace had a job and bills to pay, and surely, Gerard wouldn't postpone another minute. Helen held the phone, as heavy as a thirty-pound weight, next to her chest. "So, this is where the wind blows, Sylvia," she said as she fought back the tears she knew must eventually come.

Later that night, Helen sat on the pull-out bed, brushing her hair, with Perdita snuggled up beside her. Cat had surprised them with a picnic basket full of goodies—brie cheese, crackers, salami, fresh pears, and of course, a bottle of champagne.

"A small wedding gift from us," Cat had said as she bade them goodnight.

Helen was touched by the gesture. It was something Sylvia might have done, but Sylvia was gone, and Helen wasn't even sure if they should get married in the morning. She needed to call Grace and tell her of Sylvia's passing. She needed to call Yale and extend her leave. And Jack O'Toole to look after the house. She yanked at her hair, unconsciously. Gerard laid his hands on hers.

"You are going to pull it all out," he said. "I'm not sure how I feel about being married to a bald woman, though of course, some women look quite attractive bald. Wasn't there that one young actress who shaved her head and was really quite stunning? Of course, if you have cancer then there really isn't an option is there? … I'm blathering." He stopped talking.

Helen knew he was just trying to lift her spirits, but she felt irritated by his ability to ignore the circumstances.

"Come," he urged her, pulling her up to her feet. "You haven't had a bite to eat, nor taken a single sip of your champagne."

Helen wanted to throw her brush at him, to tip all the food onto the floor. Couldn't he see how upset she was, how stressed she was by everything that had happened— was happening? She bit her lip to keep herself from saying something she might later regret, and purposefully brushed her hair more furiously.

After a few minutes, she turned to Gerard. "I don't think we should be married tomorrow," she said quietly. "I think we should just get in the car and drop you and Perdita at home. Then I should drive down to North Carolina by myself and take care of Sylvia's arrangements. I should make plans to be there for a long time. That's what I should do."

Gerard, who had been sitting on the bed with Perdita, walked into the bathroom and shut the door. Helen listened as he relieved himself, the long, steady stream of a racehorse, then washed his hands effusively, and finally emerged. He walked over to her and took the brush out of her hands, held her hands that were cold as ice, and brushed them with his lips. "Someone wise once told me, 'you mustn't *should* on yourself.' That's a pile of 'should' you've got going on there."

"Oh, don't be clever," Helen said, pulling her hands away. "I'm feeling very stressed, pulled in many directions."

"Let's see," Gerard crossed his arms over his chest. "I want to marry you. You have a fantastic job. You live in a beautiful little house by the Sound. Your daughter adores you, and your granddaughter will. What are you stressed about? Your friend died. She was eighty years old, and she died. Sounds like life to me."

"But you are not the one who has to—" Helen began.

"Oh, but I am!" Gerard interrupted. "I am the one who left his job, his childhood home, his country to be with the woman he loves. I am the one who will be by your side as you deal with Sylvia's burial and estate, if necessary. And I will be there when you are eighty years old and making foolish decisions. I am the one who, tomorrow, will take vows to love, honor, cherish, respect, and, sometimes, just put up with you because I love you. We will be married tomorrow, Helen, and we will put things in their proper perspective. I am sorry your friend died. I am sorry you have to interrupt your work. But honestly, between us, we have so much money, we could pay someone to settle Sylvia's estate, you could resign today from your job, I could never work again, and we would still be fine! So that stress you feel is unnecessary. The only thing you should do is marry me in the morning!"

Helen was dumbfounded. She had never heard Gerard express himself so forcefully. On the one hand, she was irritated he was treating her like a petulant child; on the other, she found his determination to be quite sexy. She loved that he cared enough about her, about their relationship, to stand up and roar. Her ex-husband Frank had certainly never done that. *Screw Frank. No, screw Gerard!* Helen thought to herself as she wrapped her arms around Gerard's neck and whispered in his ear. "Of course, I will marry you in the morning. Nothing could make me happier."

She sealed her promise with a lingering kiss.

Chapter 16

January 18, 2020

*T*he next morning, Helen stood at the bedroom window looking out at a silky, blue sky and dazzling sun bouncing off the fields of pristine white snow that sparkled like the diamonds in her engagement ring.

"You are a vision of loveliness," Gerard murmured as he came up behind her and put his hands on her waist. "Should I be seeing you before the ceremony?"

"Hard not to. We are driving together," Helen laughed. "I hope you aren't disappointed that I'm not wearing white."

"Given the circumstances, I think orange is the perfect color."

"It's not orange, you lout, it's coral. If you must know, it is a vintage Coco Chanel that Sylvia gave me a few years ago. She wore it when she first met her husband, Henry. She said it brought her luck. It seemed appropriate to wear it today since …." Helen stopped, tears welling up in her eyes.

Gerard kissed the top of her head. "It's a beautiful tribute to a dear friend. Are you ready? The office opens at nine."

❊

The licensing office looked more like a five-and-dime than a government building, but the employees were super-efficient. In less than fifteen minutes, all the information was recorded, typed up, and Helen and Gerard were legally man and wife. Helen felt let down. She hadn't been expecting sparklers and a professional quartet, but these few minutes that were devoted to one of the biggest moments in her life left her feeling hollow and unfulfilled. Nevertheless, she put on a happy face for Gerard, who was beside himself, shaking everyone's hands, and threw the little bouquet Cat had sent with them over her shoulder and into the arms of an older Mexican woman who was sweeping the floors.

Once she caught the flowers, the old woman shook her head and threw the bouquet back to Helen, saying "Oh, no! No! No!" to the rest of the spectators' amusement.

Gerard took Helen by the hand and led her out of the shabby building, waving the license over his head like a trophy, and smiling, smiling, as the on-lookers' shouts of "Congratulations" disappeared into the air.

"Where are we going?" a rather subdued Helen asked as Gerard led her down the icy sidewalks, past stores of discount hunting clothes, pawn shops, and CBD vendors. The town, under restoration, was a contradiction of upscale coffee shops and boarded buildings, typical for a small New England town feeling the effects of a ragged economy. As they passed the Dunkin on the corner, the sugary, yeasty smell penetrated the air and made Helen's stomach, which was quite empty, rumble.

"Would you like something to sweeten your mood?" Gerard asked.

"My mood is just fine, thank you," Helen quipped. "Now where in God's name are you taking me?" The wind was nipping at her ankles and traveling up her skirt. Her toes were ice and her fingers frozen.

"Just another minute," Gerard assured her.

"Better be, or you will have an ice maiden on your hands."

Gerard laughed.

"No chance of that, my love," he replied. Suddenly, they found themselves in front of a gray stone church with a cheery red door. *St. Alban's Episcopal Church*, the gilded sign on the lawn read. The church was surrounded by a pretty courtyard, now blanketed in snow. Tall pine trees laden with cones swayed slightly in the wind.

"Let's go in, shall we? Say a little wedding blessing?" Gerard offered.

"It's probably locked," Helen protested, but Gerard was already up the steps, pulling on the massive handles. Miraculously, the door opened. He looked at his bride, raised his shoulders, and grinned. Holding out his hand to Helen, he led her inside.

The church was lovely, warm, and filled with the smells of incense and pine. At the end of the pews, candles were lighted. Helen was reminded of the little church in Cambridge where she had gone after her former beau, Webb, died. The little girl shouting, "Hallelujah!" The kind couple who had invited her to stay with them. It all seemed a lifetime ago—and it was. But she was here now, in this church in Vermont that was partially filled with worshippers no doubt just waiting for the priest.

"Let's go," she whispered to Gerard. "There's a service underway."

"Not yet," Gerard smiled. And suddenly, from nowhere, Grace appeared with a wreath of coral roses and baby's breath attached to a veil she had placed on Helen's head, then kissed her mother on the cheek as she pulled the veil down to cover her face. Gerard had marched ahead and stood at the front of the church next to a handsome priest who wore shiny white vestments etched with gold.

"Grace?" Helen exclaimed, dumbfounded. "What is going on?"

"Silly mommy. You are getting married!" Grace laughed. "You ready?"

On that cue, the organ music began, not the traditional wedding march but "All You Need is Love" without the full orchestra of *Love, Actually*. Helen began to tear up.

"Don't cry, Mommy. You will ruin your makeup," Grace said as she walked her mother gently down the aisle.

As Helen made her way toward Gerard, she caught glimpses of the people sitting in the congregation. There were Micah and David right up front, in their bowties. And, of course, Jake with Frankie who wore a buttercup yellow, frothy dress. And beside them, Jake's parents! And Gloria, her old next-door neighbor who had a proclivity for flashy outfits and booze. She had taken a seat next to Jack O'Toole, who looked uncomfortable as she chatted away at him non-stop. Jack had cleaned up nicely. And Abigail, now quite pregnant, and Mike, along with some of their other Habitat for Humanity friends, had shown up too. There were some ladies whom she assumed were from the flower guild, and a beautiful job they had done. It wasn't a large gathering, but Helen was touched that somehow Gerard—and probably Grace—had orchestrated all this without her knowing, that everyone had made the effort to come. The only ones missing from her cadre were Roy and Lou, other former neighbors, but they were in California. She could hardly expect them to appear at an impromptu ceremony. In lieu of their presence, however, they had sent a rather resplendent floral arrangement that blessed them in front of the altar.

The priest motioned for Helen to stand facing Gerard, to take his hands. She leaned forward to kiss the man she loved, but the priest interrupted the embrace. "Not yet," he said, sternly, with a twinkle in his eye. Everyone laughed.

"Dearly beloved, we come together in the presence of God to witness and bless the joining of this man and this woman in Holy Matrimony …" the priest intoned in his wonderfully deep voice. Helen didn't hear much after that, just a buzzing flurry of sounds that led to the inevitable question: "Helen, will you have this man to be your husband, to live together in the covenant of marriage? Will you love him, comfort him, honor, and keep him, in sickness and in health and, forsaking all others, be faithful to him as long as you both shall live?"

Helen felt the blood rush to her ears and race to her heart as she blurted out, "I will."

In a matter of minutes, Gerard had said his vows, they exchanged rings, the priest granted them the longed-for kiss, and they practically ran down the aisle, hand in hand, only to kiss once more, passionately, while their guests greeted them with whistles and applause. The only thing that could have made Helen happier was if Sylvia were there.

"You are too good to me," Helen said as she nuzzled Gerard's neck.

"Just good enough, I think," he smiled. "Let's get brunch. I am starving."

She knew her heart was sealed with his forever.

The wedding party, really everyone who had attended the service, was invited to breakfast at the local diner, The Grumpy Hen. Ten booths and the counter just accommodated the crowd, with extra space reserved for the regulars whose noses would be put out by a foreigner with money who had taken away their favorite stools. Helen ordered blueberry pancakes, while Gerard focused more heavily on sausage, bacon, eggs, and hash browns. His appetite for food—and more—was considerable. They played all the romantic music they could find on the jukebox. When the Glenn Miller Band struck up *In the Mood,* Gerard reached over and took Helen by the hand. Gathering her in his arms, he danced her down the tight aisle of the tiny diner and back while the locals watched in amusement. When the song was done, and the wedding couple had sat down, everyone clapped.

"You will have to excuse us," Gerard announced in his booming voice, his Welsh accent as thick as butter on a waffle. "We have just been married, and I am the happiest man on Earth!"

The spectators clapped again and raised their coffee mugs in congratulations. Helen, who had turned a robust shade of red, hid her face in her napkin. She heard Sylvia asking, "Does he really love you, pet?" Helen could honestly say she knew he did.

Reaching out to take his hand, she kissed his ring.

"I'm not the bloody Pope, darling. Far from it. I have too many wicked thoughts in my head to warrant veneration. And

I plan on sharing them with you as soon as we are quietly, blissfully alone."

Helen just shook her head at her husband. "You are too much."

"Just enough, I believe."

Just then, Gloria came sashaying up to the couple. "Introduce me to this handsome man. I'll say you have done very well for yourself, Helen. Surely beats the stiff you were married to before."

Helen winced, but Gerard seemed amused.

He took Gloria's hand in his and kissed it lightly. "Gerard Ferguson at your service, ma'am."

"Oh my God," Gloria shrieked. "And he has an accent too. What are you, British? Is he British, Helen?"

"Welsh," Helen replied.

"You're not moving overseas, are you? Please tell me, 'no.' I have got to have you out to the house. We will have tea. What is it you Brits say, 'a spot of tea'? I visited England once. It was so cozy. But that driving drove me crazy."

Gerard put his hand on Helen's back. "It has been a pleasure meeting you, Gloria. I look forward to that tea. Now, I fear we must mingle with the rest of our guests before we disappear."

"Naturally. Naturally. You're a lucky dog, Helen, but I always knew you had it in you." With a wink and a wiggle, she was gone.

With Vermont just a sweet memory behind them, and promises made to return, Helen and Gerard made their way back to Connecticut. Heeding her husband's advice—how foreign but pleasing did that sound!—Helen decided to take things more slowly, not to dive back into the fray.

Outside her window, the Taconic Parkway was magical, the tall evergreens frosted with snow. Deer stood like perfect ornaments beside the road, still except for the young ones' tails which flipped and twitched, flashing dark then white. Gerard had found a radio station that was playing Andrea Bocelli, whose rich voice sent goosebumps up Helen's spine. She wasn't cold, just thrilled and serene. The whole scene reminded her of a quote by J.B. Phillips Grace had shared with her not too long ago, something about frantic efforts and hysterical challenges. She wished she could remember the whole thing but no matter. She was opting for peace.

The "game plan," as Gerard put it, was to spend the night at home, *their* home, and then, tomorrow, make some phone calls to assess the situation with Sylvia's arrangements.

"Who knows?" Gerard said as he sprayed fluid on the windshield and wiped the salt away from the glass. "Maybe you won't even be needed."

"I am going to the funeral no matter what," Helen bristled.

"What if Sylvia didn't want a funeral? What if she requested to be cremated and have her ashes disposed of in some ecological way?" Gerard asked, the devil's advocate.

"Then, I will distribute her ashes. And anyway, I'm sure she would want to be buried by Henry," Helen stated firmly.

"Where is Henry buried? Did you visit a gravesite?"

An image of the urn on the fireplace mantel flashed through Helen's mind. Hadn't Sylvia said that was Henry, whom she had loved all these years? Maybe Gerard was right. Maybe she wasn't needed to arrange a funeral. Or even to sell the contents of the home. That was really up to the executor of the will. She had somehow assumed Sylvia would turn to her—but why? They were acquaintances, friends even, but Helen was nothing particularly special to Sylvia. Surely, she would have turned to someone else.

"I think a few phone calls would clear things up," Gerard said quietly. "And just because she may not have chosen you as her executor does not mean she didn't love you dearly. You and Grace. But especially you. You were her special friend."

Helen felt tears begin to well up in her eyes. "In quietness and confidence shall be our strength, not in frantic efforts and hysterical challenges," Helen whispered.

"Say again, love?" Gerard asked.

"Just something Grace told me a while ago. It seems helpful today. That's all."

Gerard reached over with one hand and placed it on Helen's, which were bunched around a soggy tissue.

They drove on.

Chapter 16

January 19, 2020

When Helen finally connected with the detective in charge of Sylvia's case, she learned they had found the will, and Helen had not been named as executor. In fact, there was no executor. Sylvia had left the contents of her house and the little savings she had to St. Michael's, the Episcopal church in town. She had deeded them the title to her home, opened her doors to them, asking only that they oversee her cremation, mix her ashes with Henry's, and then have someone take them to a beautiful place, any place—she wasn't sentimental—where the wind could take them, scatter them as it would.

"So, you won't be needing me then?" Helen asked when the detective was done.

"It wouldn't seem so," he responded.

"I would be happy to spread the ashes."

"That's a long way for you to come down, ma'am."

"She was a friend," Helen choked a little on her words.

"Suit yourself. Father Martin is perfectly willing."

Helen paused for a moment. "So, there will be no services."

"None requested."

"She is just gone."

"It appears that is what she wanted. I'm sorry for your loss."

Those words sounded so empty to Helen who had lost so many in the past few years. Frank. Webb. Well, maybe not so many, but so significant. Now Sylvia. How could she grieve? How could she mourn? Without closure, the ache would be like a knife slice on a finger, throbbing.

"Will there be anything else, ma'am?" the detective asked.

"No, thank you. You have been most helpful," Helen grimaced as she hung up the line.

She walked into the living room where Gerard sat reading, one arm resting over Perdita who lay on the couch beside him.

He looked up over the top of his tortoise-rimmed glasses. "Any luck?"

"You could say that, I suppose," Helen began. "Sylvia is all taken care of. I don't need to do a thing."

"Excellent news! What about the funeral?"

"That's just it. She didn't want one. She is to be cremated and dispersed with her late husband."

Gerard waited for Helen to continue.

Finally, she opened up, in a rush of tears. "It's not fair! Not to allow for closure."

"Why don't you have your own service here?" Gerard suggested, lovingly, but Helen plowed on ahead.

"Sylvia was not a selfish woman. I didn't think she was anyway, until now." Helen caught herself up short. "Wait, what was that you just said?"

"Why don't you have your own service here? To say goodbye. You don't need ashes, you just need friends. Grace."

"And Micah and Nicholas. They knew Sylvia." Helen leaned over and gave Gerard a kiss. "You are brilliant! I knew there was some reason I married you."

"You mean it wasn't just this?" he said, placing her hand on the thickening member inside his pants.

"Well, of course, that too!" she giggled, tumbling down into his lap.

Chapter 17

January 21, 2020

*T*hey stood in a circle on the beach—Helen, Gerard, Grace, Jake, Nicholas, and Micah, with Frankie tucked in a "snugglie" on Gerard's chest. They kept the circle small and tight to prevent the wind from blowing them all over, as the snow fell and coated the blond sand, and the whipping waves crashed against the shore. Great clouds of sea foam had massed on the shore and tumbled down beside them.

Whose idea was this anyway? Helen thought, wiggling her toes in her lined boots to keep them from freezing. It was Gerard's. Gerard who had orchestrated their lovely wedding. Gerard who had helped her to slow down. Gerard who had sung this morning in the shower a song by Flanders and Swan about the snow in January and the freezing rain in February. At least she had taken Gerard's advice not to wear the Coco Chanel suit, but rather a pair of fleece-lined trousers and a turtleneck. She was glad she was in them now.

Helen wondered what Sylvia would think, maybe even was *thinking* about all of this. The six them gathered in the freezing cold, paying tribute to her.

I'd say get your asses inside before you freeze to death, Helen heard Sylvia say. *There's nothing you can say now that hasn't been said already.*

But was that true? Had she told Sylvia how much she loved her, was indebted to her? Sylvia had been the link, the key, the angel who turned Helen's life around.

Nonsense. I am no angel. That was all you, pet. You were open to change. You know what they say, "When the pupil is ready, the teacher will appear."

Sylvia had taught Helen so many things. She had taught Helen how to be generous, not just with possessions but with time. And attention. She had taught the younger woman how to listen with both her ears and her heart. She had taught her how to stand up for herself, how to follow what she believed in. She had taught her how to love herself and others. Helen smiled as she reflected on the magical Christmas at Sylvia's house and her joy of giving.

Helen let go of Gerard's hand and wiped away the tears that were now falling. She hoped the others would assume the tears were brought on by the wind. But Helen knew better. These were tears shed because she had lost a dear teacher and friend. A woman who was irreplaceable.

"Mom," Grace nudged her, "you're up."

Helen pulled a sheet out of her pocket and began to read the words from a poem by Clare Harner Lyon:

Do not stand at my grave and weep,
I am not there. I do not sleep.
I am a thousand winds that blow.
I am the diamond glints on snow.
I am the sunlight on ripened grain.
I am the gentle autumn's rain.
When you awaken in the morning's hush,
I am the swift uplifting rush
Of quiet birds in circled flight
I am the soft stars that shine at night.
Do not stand at my grave and cry.
I am not there. I did not die.

Helen folded the paper and put it back in her pocket. Turning to the small group of friends, she began, "Sylvia was many things—a teacher, a mentor, a wife, a friend but most of all, she was a scientist. She didn't believe that death was an end but rather a beginning. Sylvia isn't ashes left behind. She is in the water, the snow, the wind, the apple tree in her backyard. She is in our hearts. I was privileged to know her, to have her as a friend. And I will miss her deeply. But I know I only have to look as far as my heart to hear her guiding me still."

Helen nodded at Grace who opened the picnic basket resting on the sand. In it were six glasses, a container of eggnog, and a bottle of whiskey. Grace handed out the glasses and filled them with the spiked drink. Helen recalled the Christmas she and Grace had spent with Sylvia, how she welcomed them into her home with eggnog and whiskey.

"To Sylvia," Grace said, raising her glass when everyone was served.

"To Sylvia," they responded in unison, then chugged their drinks.

"Now, let's get out of the cold and back to the fire," Gerard suggested as he placed the empty glasses in the basket, latched it up, and headed for home. But not without pulling Helen in to him close, as close as could be despite the large lump Frankie made on his chest, and kissing Helen's moist cheek. "Well done, dearest. Sylvia would have been pleased."

Chapter 18

January 22, 2020

*H*elen sat on her bed, looking at her nails. She needed a manicure. How had she let this go so long? The half-moons of her cuticles were peeking out beneath the red varnish she had selected for her wedding day. She scolded herself for being so negligent. *But wait*, she told herself, *don't judge yourself so harshly*. Look at all that had gone on in the past two months—Frankie's birth, Frank's death, their marriage, Sylvia's death. Certainly, she couldn't be faulted for neglecting her nails. But, she decided, she would make sure she took care of them tomorrow.

No, today, she heard Sylvia say. *There is no time like the present.*

"Is this what life is going to be like, Syl? You in my head giving me directions?"

"Who are you talking to?" Gerard asked as he entered the room.

"Oh, you know, no one. Myself. Sylvia, if you must know."

He nodded his head, understanding.

"I think I will go into town and get my nails done."

"In this storm?" Gerard asked, concerned. "Have you even looked outside? We're in the middle of a blizzard. It's a good thing the kids arrived before it hit."

"I sort of knew that when I asked them for dinner yesterday. Their apartment is so small and dreary. And cold." Helen sighed. "Oh, darling, I'm ready for daffodils and summer dresses."

"This is New England," Gerard remarked, sensibly. "Don't get your hopes up."

"Don't remind me. I'm so cold. My blood feels like ice running through my limbs, and my fingers are frozen. I guess I'll ask Grace to do my nails."

"I know the perfect way to warm up," Gerard smiled wickedly.

"I thought you would never ask."

Later, they sat in bed, holding hands as the wind whistled outside the bedroom window, and snow continued to shower down.

"Kids napping?" Gerard asked.

"Grace and Frankie, I think. Last time I saw Jake, he was reading in the library." They listened for sounds from downstairs, but all they heard was the weather doing the weather's thing. "Such a devastating loss to have them both laid off at the same time," Helen stated.

"To be fair, his funding ran out …." Gerard said.

"You mean, was snatched away by this greedy, senseless administration." Helen bristled. "Imagine not supporting bee research! Bees are the most important creatures on the planet!"

"Grace must have been livid when the government pulled the purse strings on her ESL programs too," Gerard commented.

"Though to be fair, she did ask for extended maternity leave," Helen remarked.

"But aren't they lucky to have us, you, this house, a place to stay to get their lives back in order?"

Helen was quiet. "They can't stay here forever, you know. This is my sanctuary, our sanctuary, not some hostel where anyone can just drop in and stay for a few months."

"Helen, you can't mean that." Gerard stroked her hair and nibbled her neck.

"You know I don't. It's just that I am so tired of all this shit happening. And I don't mean in our lives, I mean in the world. It seems that everyone has gone mad and reactive. Where are those days of love and peace?"

"Right here, darling, they are right here."

Helen turned suddenly, spilling Gerard in a heap beside her. "I have an idea! Why don't I just quit school once and for all? We can run off to a tropical island where we can lie naked in the sun and drink outrageously large rum cocktails. The kids can have the house as long as they need while we become ferociously healthy living on fresh fish and mangoes and swimming all day. Except when we are making love, of course. Doesn't that sound Heavenly?"

This fantasy grabbed Gerard's attention. He had long dreamed of taking Helen on a trip—and not just a fifteen-day cruise on the Rhine. He wanted to take her someplace warm—hot even—with bright blue water and fish, lots of colored fish. He had contemplated one of those bungalows with glass bottoms or a fancy shack beside the sea. Anywhere far from here, New England, with all its attachments and duties, responsibilities and claims. He wanted to whisk her away to somewhere exotic where she would forget, temporarily, about Sylvia and Grace and even Frankie. He wanted to rent a beautiful sailboat and set out for the sun. But then, he was no sailor, and he was fairly sure Helen wouldn't take kindly to being afloat. He didn't want her nervous and uncomfortable, he wanted her relaxing in an infinity pool with a fruit drink so when she emerged, like Venus rising, he could take her in his arms, and they would make fantastic love.

"What are you thinking with that mischievous grin on your face?" she asked him.

"I am wondering if you are serious. About just going somewhere."

"Half," she replied honestly.

"What would it take to get you all in?"

"A miracle," she laughed.

Gerard felt his hopes dashed.

Helen laid her hand on Gerard's arm. "But that's already happened, hasn't it? Ever since Sylvia died, all I can think is how fleeting and precious life is. I think she wants me to let go and move on."

Gerard didn't quite get the connection between her dead friend giving her advice and his image of Helen in a sexy, black, one-piece suit painted to her tan body, but he was willing to go with it, to follow her down this path. "Go on," he encouraged her.

"I am just starting to enjoy my life! I don't feel the need to be Yale's renowned Shakespeare scholar anymore. Let someone younger pick up the reins. I am through."

"Really?" Gerard could not believe what he was hearing. He felt his mood brightening as Hope blossomed on the horizon. "That's fantastic!"

"Yes, it is, isn't it! I'm done with all that. I'm ready to have adventures with my very sexy husband. Who knows, maybe I'll write a book or something."

Gerard didn't want to remind her she had already done that and might want to try something new. He took her face in his hands and gave her a long, lingering kiss.

"You know, Helen Ferry Ferguson, you are my favorite mystery. I never know what you are going to do next," he whispered in her ear.

"I just go where the wind blows me, darling. You will have to try to keep up."

Once Helen had firmly made up her mind and contacted her department head to submit her resignation, an announcement that was met with less surprise than Helen had hoped for, plans fell into place quickly. First, there was the question of Perdita and the house. She and Gerard were planning to be away for three months, beginning January 28. Helen didn't feel comfortable having Perdita kenneled for so long. In addition, there was the expense, though Gerard kept telling her to stop thinking about money. And the house ....

"No problem, Mom," Grace said, coming to the rescue. "We would love to stay here. In fact, we were sort of counting on it." Grace and Jake still lived in the one-bedroom apartment in a somewhat-shady environment. They were finding it close quarters since Frankie arrived. With Perdita, the space would seem even smaller.

"Are you sure? What about Jake?"

"Are you kidding? There's no place he would rather be than by the beach. Besides, this will give us time to think about what we want to do next. We'll save about five thousand dollars which we can put toward our next place."

"You're going to break your lease?"

"It's up at the end of the month. Didn't I tell you?"

No, Helen thought, *you didn't tell me,* and just smiled.

"We thought maybe we could store our stuff in your shed. If there's room."

"That's fine," Helen agreed, surprising herself with her own acceptance of the situation. "Thank you, darling, so much. It will only be ninety days."

"Just long enough to change a habit."

"Exactly."

"Are you sure, Mom?"

"What do you mean?" Helen asked.

"Well, you aren't going to go all Jimmy Buffett on us, are you? Seduced by rum swizzles and sunshine, never to return?"

Helen laughed. The thought had crossed her mind. But she knew herself well enough to know three months of lying around in the sun, honeymooning, swimming in the infinity pool that looked out over the blue ocean, and the islands rising like wizards caps from the sea, bird watching the banana gits, and drinking rum would be more than enough for her.

"Don't worry, sweetheart," Helen reassured her daughter. "I am like Arnold. 'I'll be back.'"

Chapter 19

January 28, 2020

elen was as good as her word. She gave her resignation
and flew off to the islands with Gerard in tow. They
had landed in the old, open-aired, pink stucco airport
on Saint Croix on the afternoon of January 28 and never
looked back. When they dismounted from the American
Airlines jet onto the runway, Helen was disappointed by
how dismal and drab everything looked. They had arrived
in a third-world country. But soon enough, she found the
wind and eighty-degree weather enchanting. As they drove
up the pot-hole etched roads, Helen was breathless with
the lush greenery, the bougainvillea, and the hibiscus. The
crowning moment came when they arrived at the villa they
had rented in the hills, just past the Karambole tide pools.
Full of light and equipped with an outdoor infinity pool, the
villa had everything they needed for a relaxed stay, including
a housekeeper named Lucia.

A few days later, they had taken to lying on the brightly-colored chaises next to the infinity pool, drinking tall, fruity drinks with umbrellas. They had quickly fallen into the pattern of taking a walk to the tidal pools in the morning and resting with a drink later in the day. At sunset, she and Gerard would make their way to the beach in the evenings to watch the glorious sunsets that outshone themselves every day. They had heard rumors the virus called COVID might send them home, but, for now, the sun beat down on Helen's bare shoulders but not fiercely so. Any discomfort she might have felt was immediately assuaged by the cool breeze that enfolded her and set the huge palm leaves in the trees beside her shaking in the wind. *They sound rather like dogs' ears when they are shaking after a bath*, thought Helen, *only more like plastic rubbing against each other*. She laughed at how poetical she had become in the short days since she and Gerard had arrived in Saint Croix.

She still felt a residue of guilt at having walked away from her career. *But no!* she thought. *Let someone else grade all those papers, prepare lectures, get up at the crack of dawn.* They had been offered the option of having daily breakfast served, but Gerard declined for them both, wanting their time on the island to be both intimate and authentic. And so, they decided to shop for fresh fish daily and feast on a variety of tropical fruits, roasted chicken, and fish. A friend had told them about a fresh lobster "stand" where the boats pulled up to the road and let the lobsters out. They went there, picked the two largest lobsters they could find, and the lobstermen prepared them. Then Helen and Gerard sat down at a picnic table and ate a delicious and juicy meal, laughing and smiling as butter ran down their chins.

Helen thought, *This is the most romantic meal of my life.*

"You good?" Gerard asked.

"The best," Helen said, shoving more fresh meat into her mouth.

Chapter 20

February 8, 2020

"Well?" Grace texted Helen. "Is it as good as you hoped for?"

"Better. That's all I am going to say."

On the way back through town, Helen's sandals flapped as she walked, tossing sand and pebbles up the backs of her legs. But not unpleasantly so. It could have been snow. And sleet. Grace had texted her that New England had just been hit by a giant winter storm. She had called Jack O'Toole to restock the wood, and the handyman had been keeping the driveway plowed, though Jake had opted to stay at home and job hunt in front of the fire. So, it was all a happy family with them.

At the market, which only met on Saturday morning, Helen filled her net bag with limes, plantains, bora, coconuts, and greens.

"What is this one?" Gerard asked the woman with the gleaming white teeth who stood behind the table.

"Starfruit. Very juicy. Refreshing."

Helen's ears perked up. She walked over by Gerard as the woman took the rubbery-looking yellow fruit in one palm and cut it into several thick slices, handing them each one.

"I love these! I have had them before," Helen said as she bit into her slice. "They really are so refreshing."

"Delicious!" Gerard concurred, the juice from the sweet fruit dribbling down his chin. "We will have five please!"

The woman laughed and picked out five perfect fruits. As she handed them to Helen, who placed them gently in her bag, a little boy, probably no more than three years old, peeked out from behind the women's skirts.

"Hello!" Gerard smiled. "What's your name?"

The woman put her hand on the top of the child's head. He gathered up her skirts and shoved them in his mouth. The woman swatted him away. "Dat's Remi. Don't mind him," the woman said as she handed Gerard the change.

"He's adorable," Helen remarked. "How old?"

"Three."

"I have a granddaughter who is almost seven weeks old. Her name is Frankie."

"Frankie?" the woman asked with arched eyebrows. "The man's name?"

Helen laughed, nodding. "She was named after her grandfather who died the day she was born."

"Where they get these names from," the woman said, shaking her head. "My daughter name him Remi Martin after some fancy drink she like."

Gerard bit into one of the starfruits. "Yes, that's a very fine cognac."

"It so fine, it killed her," the woman continued. "That and the drugs. Now, I got no baby. Just a grandbaby named Remi Martin."

Helen felt a well of sorrow fill inside her for the woman who was saddled with a responsibility she didn't ask for, but which she could not refuse. How many like her were there, not just on this tiny island but all over America? The world? "It must be difficult having to care for him and run your own business," Helen said.

"It is."

Gerard could sense where this was going. Helen had been on the island for eleven days, relaxing, and now she was starting to get the itch, the old itch, to *do something*. She was starting down the road to salvation, in her compassion, reaching out to stragglers along the way. The last thing Gerard wanted was to find himself in the wings, doing Sudoku, while Helen babysat for a three-year-old for two-and-a-half months. He put his hand firmly on her back and led her away from the stall, leaving a generous tip.

"Thank you, sir," the old woman grinned. He just waved his free hand as they walked away.

"You know, I don't appreciate your doing that," Helen remarked angrily.

"Doing what? Saving my honeymoon from Saint Helen?"

"What do you mean?"

"You were about to invite that child to move in with us for the next two-and-a-half months!"

"I was not!"

"Helen," Gerard penetrated her defenses.

"Oh, all right. I was going to offer to babysit. She was so nice. He was so cute. She needs help."

"Helen, you are acting like an imperialist, assuming that you have the answers to other people's non-problems."

It occurred to Helen this was the first argument she and Gerard had engaged in since they were married. She wasn't going to back down, though she wasn't entirely sure why. "That woman needed help. We have time and money," she stated.

"Time and money for us," Gerard replied.

"Well, that is selfish!"

"What is selfish is if you throw yourself at that child's life for three months because it makes you feel good about yourself. Then you disappear? What happens to the child then?"

Helen was taken aback. Is that what she was doing? Making herself feel better? Atoning for the guilt she felt for leaving Grace and Frankie behind, quitting her job, living off Gerard's money? Did everything always have to be so layered? This she knew: Gerard was very smart and perceptive. He seemed to know her better than she knew herself. So, she would listen to him, ask his advice, heed what he had to say. It made her toes curl to do this, but do this she must if she was going to continue to change. Besides, she trusted him (mostly) to say the loving thing.

"So, what do you suggest we do?" she asked sincerely.

"Quite simple. Either we leave them alone entirely, or we offer to adopt Remi and take him back to the States with us."

Helen's heart almost exploded. *Adopt him? Adopt Remi!* She was in her sixties, recently retired, and newly married. What would she want with raising a baby at this point in her life?

Frankie was different. Helen could always send her home to her mom and dad after a long day, but a three-year-old boy who would be calling her "Mama" and Gerard "Papa" for the rest of their days? And yet, how could she abandon Remi completely? That seemed so harsh and unforgiving. Maybe there was another way. "Couldn't we just start a preschool or something? Somewhere where the kids can go to get a good start?"

Gerard kissed the top of Helen's head. "Can't this be a honeymoon, not a crusade?"

Helen wondered why it was so difficult to just relax and have fun. Why did she feel this compulsion to share their blessings with those less fortunate than they were? *Damn it, Sylvia*, she thought to herself. *You have done it … again.*

The villa they had rented was high on a hill overlooking the harbor that was dotted with elegant sailboats and heftier speed boats and yachts. After their trudge up the dusty road to the house, the housekeeper, Lucia, a middle-aged woman whose face was etched with lines, met them with glasses of freshly-squeezed lime juice, a refreshment Gerard wondered how he had ever survived without. Lucia giggled, her eyes crinkling, twinkling. Despite Helen's protestations, Gerard had hired the woman to come every morning to make beds, sweep up, and prepare something for dinner later on.

"It will be a proper vacation," he told Helen, who reminded him they would have company every morning, intruding on their intimate space. "There will be plenty of time for that," he winked. "I would just like you to be a wee bit pampered."

"A wee bit pampered?" Helen asked skeptically.

"That's Welsh for foreplay. I could have said I would like

to make sure you are rested up so that we could enjoy a good fuck—" he began.

"Wee bit pampered will do," Helen interrupted.

The newlyweds sat on the patio in padded rattan chairs while Lucia worked her magic with the fish they had brought from the market. The smells of aromatic spices and lemon wafted through the villa and out to the couple as they sat gazing out at the ultra-blue water and the islands beyond.

"This is perfect," Helen said, taking Gerard's hand. She was watching the birds wheel in the sky below them, circling and diving like miniature kites. Up on the hill, the breeze was strong and the air cool, though the temperature had been at least ten degrees warmer below in the market.

Helen closed her eyes. *This is perfect, being here with Gerard, being married to Gerard*, she admitted to herself. He brought out the youth and adventure in her, attributes she thought she had lost forever. Just yesterday, he had suggested they go waterskiing. He had rented a boat and skis and taken her out into the bay. Despite her protestations, he had convinced her, gently, to give it a go, to let the boat pull her up out of the water and onto her feet. At first, she felt excited by the idea of waterskiing, but once she was in the water, she wasn't so sure. As she held on to the handlebars, and the boat began to slowly pull away, she felt herself lock up. *I can't do this*, she told herself. *Who do I think I'm kidding?* And no sooner had that thought crossed her mind, she found herself facedown in the water.

Gerard circled the boat around and grinned. "Let's give it another go, shall we, or are you ready to give up?"

While Helen was tempted to throw in the towel, she also wanted to prove to herself and to Gerard she could, and would, keep up with him on their daring adventure.

Many attempts later, just when she was about to give up, the magic took! She let go of trying to make things happen and instead visualized herself rising from the water—Botticelli's Aphrodite on the half shell—and she did! She stayed upright for about three minutes and then came tumbling down.

"Enough!" she cried as Gerard cheered her on, bringing the boat around to retrieve her. As he hoisted her back into the boat, she was satisfied she had fulfilled his fantasy. *But what about my fantasy?* she wondered. Why was it *enough* and not *brilliant* or *I did it?* Helen knew she had to be careful not to wrap herself around Gerard's expectations and desires like a tight ribbon on a spool. That was the old way of doing things, to make everyone else happy. While she certainly wanted Gerard to enjoy himself, she had no intention of sacrificing the strides she had made toward self-actualization in order to give him joy.

"You were brilliant!" Gerard said, oblivious to her inner ruminations. "You think you can take the wheel while I have a go?"

Helen laughed. She had just succeeded in waterskiing without breaking a limb. *Now drive the boat? Are the challenges never ending?* she wondered as she gripped the wheel, something she hadn't done for twenty years since she and Frank had owned a Boston Whaler in Connecticut. *Is this about having fun or about proving something?* Did Gerard need her to prove she could keep up with him, that he needn't regret marrying a woman who was so much older?

"Honestly, Helen," Gerard said, bringing her back to the patio where they now sat drinking their lime refreshers. "This is getting tedious. You are only as old as you feel. If you keep telling yourself that you are an old woman, then you will certainly become one. And I shall have to go find another playmate to spend my enormous wealth with." He took a sip of his drink, his gaze focused outward on the idyllic scene.

Helen was taken aback. "Why, that's a horrible thing to say! That is exactly my worst nightmare!"

Gerard looked at her with love in his eyes. "You know I wouldn't do that."

"Do I?"

"You should. All I want for you to do is to be my lover, my wife, and my friend. Please, dear God, don't let the physical nature of our relationship get in the way of our mental and spiritual connection. All I want for this short time that we have together is to have fun. Play."

Helen had heard that before, from Sylvia who had even sent her a little green pin to wear on her lapel that read "Run Outside and Play." Helen knew some of her difficulty in life stemmed from taking herself too seriously and trying to control outcomes. And being so righteous about everything. All—*all*—her difficulties in life were rooted in those three.

Why did every trip she took have to turn into an opportunity to improve something? Renovate her life and the lives of those around her. Even her little house by the Sound. She had rehabbed the hell out of it, so it was barely recognizable. But wasn't it really just for the location and the view she had purchased the property to begin with? She could have saved tens of thousands of dollars if she had just been content to sit on the front porch and watch the seagulls sail above the water.

And people. Wasn't she always trying to improve people's lives? Take Gerard, for example. No! He was one who would not be rehabbed. If anything, he was knocking down old walls and building a new Helen. He was helping her tear off old wallpaper and reveal her true self.

Again, Helen said to herself, *again I will surrender and let myself be changed. I will listen and breathe and—*

"Helen?" Gerard interrupted her reveries. "I can almost feel the heat coming from your brain."

"I am just thinking."

"No shit."

"I am going to stop now." She took a sip of her juice, rose from her chair, and stood by the balcony, looking out over the landscape and water beyond.

Lucia came to the patio, wearing a small red hat and carrying a large multi-colored straw bag. "I am to home now. I will be back Monday. I left meals for two nights. Have a pleasant weekend."

Gerard rose. "Thank you, Lucia. By the way," he said raising his glass, "the limewater is delicious, as always."

"Thank you, sir," she giggled and walked away.

After the door closed, Gerard came over and stood by Helen. He put his arm around her and kissed her hair. "Yum. You smell of frangipani. So, what would you like—"

Before he could even finish his sentence, Helen pressed her lips on his. She was undoing the buttons on his flower print shirt, then pulling down his shorts.

"I like this," he said, burying his face in her neck.

"I can tell," Helen laughed back.

"Helen the Seductress. I could get used to this."

"You'd better. I am turning over a new leaf," she said as she pulled her light shirt over her head, removed her bra and panties. She stood before him, luscious and bronzed, glowing with an energy and playfulness that made Gerard desire her all the more. "Let's start in the infinity pool. After all, we have all weekend," she called to him over her shoulder as she walked outside.

Gerard followed. "Now that's the woman I married," he called out to her. "That's no old woman. That's a minx."

Chapter 21

February 26, 2020

Once Helen had embraced her new, adventuress self, life became much more fun. She told herself every morning, *I can do anything*, and then proceeded to—snorkeling at Frederiksted Pier with the sequined pier squid, boogie boarding, scuba diving. Nothing could stop her. With each new experience, she felt her soul expand. After coming in from galloping on a horse along the beach, she released her hair from its ponytail, shook her red locks free.

"I can't believe I have waited this long," she told Gerard, who stood watching her, amused.

"This long for what?" he asked.

"To enjoy life. I feel as if a rather large 'Trust' button has been installed inside me, and suddenly, I am unstoppable! Bring it on!"

"Are you sure about that?" Gerard asked.

Helen could see the twinkle in his eye. What was he up to?

"What are you thinking?" she asked him.

"How about skydiving? Would you be game to try that?"

Helen felt her heart sink into her stomach and rise again. *Skydive? Jump out of a plane?*

"It will be tandem. You would be attached to an instructor. All you would have to do is let go." That certainly made it sound easier and much more doable.

"All right then," she said. "Let's do it!"

The closer the day drew to the actual jump, the more Helen began to regret her decision. What if her blood pressure rose through the roof, and she had a heart attack? What if the parachutes didn't open, or she became loosed from her tandem partner and plummeted to the ground? Gerard, picking up on her anxiety, assured her they needn't follow through with it, but Helen was determined. She was going to go through with this, by God, but she was not going to tell Grace until she was safely on the ground.

The day came.

As they drove to the small airport, she felt her palms sweating, her heart pumping in her chest. Everything in her wanted to run away, but she just kept putting one foot in front of the other as she donned her skydiving suit and goggles, mounted the stairs to the plane, and took her seat. Before she knew it, they were traveling at what seemed like the speed of light, the door to the aircraft open. Gerard dangled his legs out, having the time of his life. She wasn't sure when he leapt because she'd had her eyes closed tight as the instructor pushed her toward the door. She clasped onto the sides of the plane, determined not to make the leap, but he pushed her out. The next thirty seconds, she felt as though something was sucking the air out of her body, and then … it was all a dream.

The parachute opened, and they rose up, only to float down, rocking over the island below. There was none of that drifting and sailing that is often shown on films when people jump out of planes. No circles of friends holding hands and singing "Kumbaya." Just Helen, hurling through space. She didn't see much. She had her eyes closed for most of the event, but she knew when the instructor told her to stick her legs out straight in front of her that they were close to landing. She felt it too, that hard bumping as they slid on the ground.

"Well, how did you like it?" Gerard asked her, beaming. "You survived!"

"Almost," she answered. "I can honestly say I have never felt anything like that."

"Want to go again?"

"Never," was her quick reply.

Gerard was having the time of his life. The more bronzed, luscious, and adventurous Helen became, the more he desired her and sought to please her by coming up with the next thrilling exploit for them to engage in. Their intimacy increased, and when they made love, they were more playful than ever before. Gerard had never had a lover like Helen—this new Helen—before. If he had ever had any thoughts of leaving her, which he had not, they were gone. He could never leave this woman who so satisfied his every desire. Nor would he want to.

The days, weeks passed in an exchange of blessings. The honeymoon was only made more perfect by the setting—the gorgeous island, temperate weather, friendly people, delicious food, and bottles of Mount Gay rum.

"I don't ever want to leave," Helen announced one day as they sat on the patio, enjoying their drinks, the view, each other. "Let's buy a place and stay here."

"You don't mean that," Gerard smiled. "You have honeymoonitis."

"Is that a thing?" Helen asked, sipping her drink.

"I believe it is. It is what happens when you are having the time of your life, and you want it to last forever."

"It's not like we couldn't afford to buy a place ...." she began.

Gerard thought for a moment. "Yes, you are right. But what if we bought a place, and it wasn't the same when we came back? I'd rather frame these memories and mount them on the wall of my mind forever. Not tarnish them with future visits."

"Gerard Ferguson, I do believe you are a romantic!"

Gerard grinned. "I come by it naturally. It's the Welsh in me."

They sat quietly, holding hands, watching the birds—their white bellies illuminated by the sun—soaring against the blue sky.

"There will be other places, Helen. I promise, we will travel to a thousand equally beautiful spots."

Helen sighed. Right now, she was happy here. But she was glad, too, that the trip was almost over. Truly, she missed her little dog and her house, her granddaughter and Grace. To Helen, it felt as if she and Gerard had been playing at something, she couldn't name what, but she was ready to dig in and get her hands into something new—meaty. Enough of this bonbon life in paradise. She was ready to start the next chapter, whatever that was. She had no job, no financial obligations. Yes, she wanted to help with Frankie, but not as a helicopter grandma. She thought perhaps she might like to write a book, fiction this time. Something juicy, maybe a mystery novel with a very complicated and mysterious protagonist. She had read in the local paper about a woman who threw herself off a cliff into the ocean. Her sister had flown down from the mainland to investigate her death. That might be a starting point. A sister story. And with her recent skydiving adventure, she felt qualified to write about throwing oneself headlong off a cliff.

"Helen? Helen, are you there? Can you hear me?"

Helen shook her head, her mane of red hair cascading down her back. "Sorry. I was just thinking."

"Well, that is obvious. What were you thinking about? It looked painful."

"I was thinking about what I would like to do next," she replied.

"I thought you wanted to buy a house and stay here forever," Gerard said, confused.

"No."

"Does it involve getting naked?" Gerard asked, hopeful.

"Not now. When we get home, what do you think about my writing a book?"

"Well, you have certainly done that before," Gerard responded, disappointed.

"A new book. Fiction. A mystery or a thriller."

"I have never quite understood the difference," Gerard said.

"Actually, I think they are synonymous. A mystery just has more puzzle to it while a thriller is more suspense."

"What is yours going to be?"

"I am not sure yet," Helen remarked as she ran her hands through her hair. "I am not even sure how to begin."

"Fair enough," Gerard said, finishing off his drink, then turning his gaze back to watch the waves crashing below them. He looked over the idyllic scene, grateful for all the blessings he was enjoying in his life—for Helen, in all her complexity; for his father's legacy that was enabling him to live the life of his dreams; for the island that had awoken something in Helen, making her more open and playful; for life in general and joy in particular. He reached over to Helen and squeezed her hand.

Helen was lost in her own thoughts, thinking about the ocean and the rocks and why a young woman would want to end her life on such a beautiful island. *If this is a metaphor for my life,* Helen told herself, *that makes sense. How someone could come to a place like this and leave their old self behind.* But she didn't want her first novel to be a metaphor. She wanted it to be real and gripping. Using the setting of this paradise, she would fashion a story full of greed, desire, and despair. *No wait,* she thought, *that is too severe. I just want to write a book about a sister who comes to an island to investigate the death of her sibling.*

"Sounds intriguing," Gerard said as he fixed himself another rum swizzle.

Helen could not wait to get home to start her project. Gerard saw the look on Helen's face and knew she had latched on to something. He also knew it meant their three months of uninterrupted pleasure was over. He might as well start packing the bags. He knew Helen well enough to know when she started something—whether it was painting a house, taking a walk, or writing a book—she engaged in the project with an intensity that would put a thoroughbred to shame. He loved this about her, admired her for it, but he had hoped the months away would have balanced her out a little, leave time for recreation, relaxation. Him.

As if reading her husband's thoughts, Helen turned to Gerard. "I have the most wonderful idea," she whispered.

"I could tell."

"You could?" she asked, surprised. "What was it?"

"You have just established the complete character list and synopsis for your book."

Helen smiled. "Actually, I was thinking of something more along the lines of this." She reached over and took his face in her hands. Then, she kissed him with conviction. They both rose, and Helen took Gerard by the hand. "I may have found a new project," she said over her shoulder, "but I will always have time for you."

Gerard looked up at the sky, smiling on his good fortune.